Gone Before Breakfast

Jan Howery

Jan-Carol
Publishing, Inc
"every story needs a book"

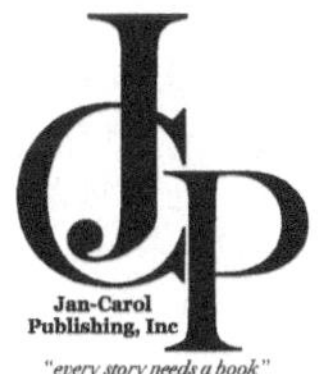

Gone Before Breakfast
Whisper Cozy Romance Mystery Series
Jan Howery
Published June 2023
Little Creek Books
Imprint of Jan-Carol Publishing, Inc.

ISBN: 978-1-954978-89-8
Library of Congress Control Number: 2023940219

You may contact the publisher:
Jan-Carol Publishing, Inc.
PO Box 701
Johnson City, TN 37605
publisher@jancarolpublishing.com
www.jancarolpublishing.com

My eighth-grade teacher, Ms. Blackwell, had no idea the impact she would have on my life or my future in a writing career when she spoke these simple words to the class after reading my classroom assignment to write a paragraph with three or four sentences describing an event or happening. "This is fantastic! Your punctuation is atrocious, but this writing is just wonderful!" she said.

It is because of her that at the early age of thirteen, I believed that I could write worthy material that people would enjoy reading. I dedicate this and my future writings to her.

Author's Note

Self-published authors and small book presses are sometimes overlooked and overshadowed by the celebrities' books and larger publishers, but these authors and the small publishers are well deserving of a best-selling book. Support local bookstores and local authors by investing their literary works.

Chapter 1

"Jackson! Come on! We're going to be late!" Jan yelled as she made her way toward the front door.

"I'm right behind you!" Jackson yelled back as he hurled himself down the stairs.

"You know, the old retiree is already moving slowly," Jan snapped with a snicker.

"Watch it! I heard that!" Jackson said as they raced through the front door and headed to the car. "Give me the keys! I'll drive there, and you can drive back."

"Where are Brandon and Allison? I thought they were meeting us here! And we're already late!" Jan asked hurriedly.

"No," Jackson quickly answered calmly. "Change of plans. They'll meet us there."

Jan tossed the keys to him and hopped in the car. Jackson got in the car when Jan looked over to him and instructed, "Wait. Your tie is crooked. Let me straighten it."

As Jan moved closer to Jackson, straightening his tie, his hand moved across her breast. "Since we're already late, we could just be a little later," he said with a boyish grin.

Jan slapped his hand away but said in a flirtatious tone, "Stop it! And look at you! You're so handsome, I'll be fighting all the women off of you tonight!"

"And you, my dear, are beautiful," Jackson whispered in her ear as he started the car and pulled out of the driveway.

The evening's event was Jackson Taylor's retirement party. Jan Foster had dated Jackson Taylor, an attorney, for about eight years. He was fifty-five years old, fifteen years older than her, but the age gap made no difference to them. They had what seemed to be the perfect relationship, though Jackson was known to be a big flirt with any and all women. Jackson worked hard and played hard. He had practiced law for twenty-five years and was now retiring from his law practice.

Jan worked full-time for a small book publishing company and loved her work. Her hours were around the clock sometimes, with deadlines, contracts, and royalty reports, but she loved the creativity and freedom in her work.

Upon arriving at the well-known The Martha Washington Inn & Spa, Jackson drove the car into the driveway.

"Look at the people!" Jan announced. "How many people did you invite?"

"It's the 'who's who' list," Jackson said proudly. "It's important for the law firm's future. And you know I'm staying on as the 'Of Counsel Attorney.' 'Gotta make sure the law firm does well!"

The valet opened their car doors, and Jackson handed him the keys. He and Jan quickly made their way up the front entrance's steps and went through the main door. Upon entering, they heard, "Here's the man of the hour! You know you're late, right?"

"Thanks, Brandon," Jackson replied as he turned toward the sound of the voice.

Brandon was Jackson's younger brother. He was at the party with his girlfriend, Allison Hurley. They had been dating for six years now. Around a year after they'd started dating, the CPA firm Allison worked for had closed its doors because the owner had suddenly died from a heart attack. Brandon owned a small landscaping company; he was great with the labor but not with managing the business. He offered Allison a job as bookkeeper and office manager. She'd reluctantly accepted, and somehow it had worked. While they'd been afraid that the everyday closeness would put a strain on their personal relationship, it ended up drawing them closer. It worked perfectly for both of them. They kept separate homes and learned to give each other their own space. They worked together and planned for the future together, both for the company and their relationship.

"Jan, you look lovely," Brandon said. "Jackson and I are with the most beautiful women here."

Allison walked up and gave Jan a hug. "Wow, you look stunning!"

"Me? Did you take a look in the mirror? You are beautiful!" Jan replied.

"Yes," Jackson interjected, "our two women are the prettiest and most sophisticated ladies here! And where's the bar? I'll get our ladies something to drink."

"Red," Jan answered quickly.

"White," Allison followed with a quick reply.

"Come on, Brandon. Let's get drinks for these magnificent ladies!"

As the brothers walked away, Allison turned to Jan and asked, "Are you excited about Jackson's retirement?"

"Well, not exactly. With him retiring, I'm afraid he'll stay gone, traveling. I can't always go with him, and I'm concerned that I'll see less of him. Less than I already do, considering all the trips he takes," Jan answered.

"But you can do a lot of your work on the road," Allison said. "You might be able to go with him more than you think."

"I guess," Jan replied, sounding doubtful. "But what I *am* excited about is our Valentine's Day trip to St. Thomas!"

"Oh, me, too! I'm already packed," Allison said with a giggle. "Think about it—two full weeks in the land of fun and sun."

Jackson and Brandon returned, interrupting their conversation.

"Ladies, here are your drinks," Jackson said.

"Jackson, the man of the hour, it's about time. Everyone is being seated," Brandon said, motioning for them to walk into the dining room.

The dinner was exquisite. Everything from the appetizers to the desserts were perfection. Presenters roasted and toasted Jackson, and there were jokes and slaps on the backs, and it was a fun atmosphere. Finally, when all of the congratulations were over, the band started playing music. People hit the dance floor and danced into the wee hours of the morning.

* * *

"Do you know what time it is?" Allison asked as she and Jan walked from the ballroom into the lobby. "I'm exhausted, but this was a lot of fun."

Brandon, who was walking behind Allison, said, "Late. I'll go get the valet to bring the car around. I sure hope you're able to drive."

"Yes," Allison answered. "I knew that I'd be the designated driver."

"Me, too," Jan interjected. "And where is Jackson?"

"I don't know," Brandon yelled over his shoulder as he walked out the door.

"That Jackson! He's probably under the table with—" Jan stopped mid-sentence when she turned and saw Jackson practically being carried down the hallway by one of the waitresses.

"What happened?!" Jan yelled, running to Jackson.

"I'm so sorry! He was dancing with a glass in his hand and fell. He's bleeding pretty badly," the waitress said, clearly panicking. "I wrapped his hand in a towel, but—"

Jan interrupted, exclaiming, "My heavens! He's bleeding profusely! Someone call 911!"

Jackson slipped his uninjured hand into his pocket and handed the waitress a wad of hundred-dollar bills. "You are the sweetest thing," he said, slurring every word. "I think that I'll—" He passed out suddenly, hitting his head on the floor before he could finish his sentence.

"Geez! Jackson! Jackson! Oh, dear lord! Get another towel!" Jan screamed.

Brandon staggered through the front door and asked, "What the hell happened? Jackson?"

"He fell. He's bleeding really badly," Allison said, trying to keep calm. "Did someone call 911?"

"Well, I guess that's why the ambulance is out front," Brandon stammered.

"Brandon! Sober up! And tell'em to get in here!" Allison yelled.

As Brandon turned and opened the door, the paramedics rushed inside. The lobby floor was covered with blood, and Jackson was unresponsive.

"His hand! He fell and cut his hand really bad!" Jan explained to them.

"Has he been drinking?" one of them asked.

"Yes, and he's drunk," Jan said almost apologetically.

"We need to get him to the ER asap!" one of the paramedics whispered as they carried Jackson out on a stretcher.

"Allison, you and Brandon meet me at the hospital. I'm riding with 'em to the hospital," Jan said.

Allison and Brandon exited the building, got in their car, and followed the ambulance to the hospital. By the time they had parked, Jan and Jackson had disappeared through the doors leading to the surgical wing.

Two hours passed before Jan came out to the visitors' waiting room. "He just got out of surgery. He cut a main artery below his thumb, like he cut his own wrist. He could have bled to death. He lost a lot of blood and they're having to give him blood. And then, of course, with all that alcohol in his blood that didn't help things. He's going to be okay, but he'll feel really bad for the next couple of days," Jan said.

"How on earth did he fall?" Allison asked.

"He was drunk," Jan answered. "And flirting and showing off in front of the waitresses. Did you see what he did? He was dying but still handed that waitress several hundred dollars! Really!"

"That's my brother," Brandon said with a snicker.

"I know. And I still love him," Jan replied, smiling.

"Well, why don't we take you to get your car from The Martha, and you go home and rest, then come back tomorrow," Allison suggested.

"Tomorrow?" Brandon asked with a smirk.

Allison and Jan ignored his remark.

"You don't need to stay here. There's nothing you can do. Go home, rest up, and come back later," Allison said. "And now that he's out of surgery, he's going to be fine."

"Okay, I guess you're right. Nothing I can do," Jan said. "I'll let the nurse know. They're getting a room prepared for him now. I do need to change clothes. I'm covered in blood."

* * *

Over the next couple of days, Jan hardly ever left Jackson's side at the hospital. She only left the hospital only to change clothes or grab a bite to eat, and then she'd be back by his side.

A few of days later, as she was walking into the hospital her cell phone rang.

"Hey, how are you doing?" Allison asked when Jan answered.

"Hi, Allison. I'm okay. Jackson is doing much better. And I think that he'll get to go home this afternoon," Jan answered.

"He should really appreciate you, Jan. You've been right there for him," Allison said.

"I'm sure he does. He has seemed so helpless the last couple of days. I think that reality hit him. He could have died!" Jan said.

"Well, he better get well soon. Our trip to St. Thomas is paid for, we have first-class tickets, and I plan to have my Valentine's Day dinner on the beach. You tell him that I said to get his ass well soon!" Allison said, laughing.

"Oh, I'll tell him. And tell Brandon that Jackson will be coming home this afternoon. He's been stopping by to check on him. If he isn't released for some reason, I'll let you know. I'm getting ready to walk into his room. Talk to you later," Jan said, then hit the end button on her phone.

"Hey, how are you doing?" Jan asked Jackson.

"They're releasing me this afternoon. After forty-five stitches, I am homebound. Worse hangover I've ever had," Jackson said with a wink.

"Serves you right!" Jan said with a smile. "Do you remember anything?"

"I remember waking up and seeing your beautiful face," Jackson said.

"Well, I guess you lost a day or two in between," Jan answered jokingly.

The nurse walked in the room, interrupting their conversation. "Mr. Taylor, are you ready to go home?"

"Yes, I am, sweetie," Jackson answered happily.

"Well, let's get your paperwork done, and you're on your way," the nurse replied, winking at Jan.

"Oh, he's definitely ready to go home," Jan said. "I'll go get the car."

Jan pulled the car to the entrance. Jackson was transported by wheelchair to the front of the building.

"Now, if I need a nurse to call, are you available?" Jackson asked the nurse with a wink.

Jan got out of the car and opened the side door for Jackson. The nurse answered, "No, Mr. Taylor. But I believe this young lady will provide all the care you need."

Jackson rose from his wheelchair and replied, "You are absolutely right!"

Chapter 2

As the day approached to leave for their two-week vacation, things were hectic for Jan at work. She raced around the clock to meet deadlines early so she wouldn't be working on vacation. She worried about Jackson, too. He was busy going to the office, completing cases, and going to physical therapy. He didn't seem to be as excited about the trip as he had been.

Jan was working late at the office when she heard her cell phone ding. It was a text from Jackson:

Jackson: Meet us Peppermill drinks dinner 30 minutes

Jan: Who?

Jackson: B A

Oh, she thought. *Brandon and Allison.*

Jackson: Final plans trip

Finalize plans? she thought. *Plans are finalized. We leave in the morning!*

Jan left and arrived at the restaurant in about forty minutes.

"Hey! We thought you'd never get here," Jackson yelled from the bar as she walked inside the lobby.

"Don't give the working girl a hard time," Brandon snapped laughing.

"That's right, Jackson," Allison said. "Just because you're retired doesn't mean the rest of us get to take it easy!"

Jan walked over to Jackson, and he gave her a kiss on the forehead and said sweetly, "Just kidding."

"I know," Jan replied.

"Don't you let him give you a rough time," Allison said with a smile. "Because if he does, we'll make him carry our luggage!"

"Yeah, I can see it now . . . with that injured hand!" Brandon said sarcastically, laughing.

"I'm starved," Jan interrupted. "Let's just eat here at the bar."

They ate their dinner, and as they walked out of the restaurant together later, Jan said, "See you all in the morning!"

"Yes, you will!" Allison answered. "And we won't be late!"

Chapter 3

The flight to St. Thomas was an easy one. They flew out of the Tri-Cities Airport in Tennessee on an early morning flight with flight connections in Charlotte, North Carolina. They were walking on the beach at the Marriott Resort in St. Thomas by mid-afternoon.

"I'm so excited to be here! Two whole weeks!" Jan said with excitement as they walked along the beach and in the water. "I thought this day would never come."

"Feel this air. Look at this water," Allison said. "I'm ready for a cocktail."

Brandon and Jackson were walking on the beach in front of the ladies, and Brandon answered, "Sounds good to me. Since we can't check into our rooms for another hour, let's make the most of it. I hear a mango drink calling my name!"

Jackson turned to Jan and said, "I would love to share a drink with the most beautiful woman in my life…and on this island! Shall we?" He reached to take her hand.

Jan blushed at the unsolicited compliment. "Yes! Take me! I'm yours!" They both giggled like school sweethearts, and the four of them made their way to the bar.

The whole trip was exciting and relaxing. The guys spent much of their time on scuba excursions, while the ladies enjoyed spa time together. It was two weeks of fun in the sun as they explored the island, visited other islands, and had lots of tasty meals. Jan joined Brandon and Jackson on a couple of their scuba diving excursions, leaving Allison to relax by the pool. But Jan decided, it was a 'boys' scuba trip and most of the time, she and Allison made it a 'girls' trip, spending their time shopping, visiting the spa, and relaxing by the pool. In the evenings, the four of them enjoyed dining at different restaurants and taking quiet strolls on the beach.

The two-week vacation went by much too quickly.

* * *

"Aren't we happy to be back in the good ol' US of A and Charlotte, North Carolina?" Jackson announced sarcastically as he stood up from his seat and waited to exit the plane.

"We had such a great vacation. I didn't want it to end," Jan replied. "We were able to actually relax and enjoy ourselves."

"I know," Allison replied. "I'm not ready to go back to work. I'm still on no work vacation island time."

"Quieten down, you two," Brandon said, winking as they deplaned. "Your noise is not working well with my hangover."

"Serves you right," Allison said loudly. "I'm starving! Let's get breakfast. We have at least a two-hour layover before our connecting flight."

"Sounds good to me," Jan agreed. "Hey, let's walk over to the connecting concourse and just eat over there."

"Girls, how do the two of you stay so thin when you eat all the time?" Jackson asked.

"Is that Whiskey River restaurant open for breakfast?" Allison asked, ignoring him.

"Yup, I think so. That's perfect," Jan said.

"Well, okay. We'll follow you ladies," Brandon said with a smile.

The restaurant was not terribly busy, and they quickly found a table for four. The girls sat down and grabbed the menus.

"You order for me, honey," Jackson said to Jan. "I'm going to find the men's room."

"Me, too," Brandon said. "Allison, I'll have whatever you are having." Brandon leaned over and kissed Allison on the top of her head.

Jackson blew a kiss to Jan, and the brothers turned and began walking down the hallway in search of a men's room.

"Hey, you can leave your luggage with us!" Jan yelled.

"They didn't hear you. They must be in a hurry to get to the men's room," Allison said giggling.

A server walked up to their table and said, "Are you ready to order?"

"Yes, we are," Jan answered.

Breakfast was ordered and served. The girls didn't wait for the brothers to return before eating. While they talked and ate, they lost track of time and didn't seem to notice that the brothers had not returned.

Abruptly, Allison said, "We've finished eating, and they're not back yet. Do you think that Brandon got sick or something?"

"Gee, I don't think so. He didn't act that sick. I'll text Jackson. Geez, their food is cold. He's probably in a bar with some flight attendant and forgot I'm sitting here!" Jan said, trying to find some humor in the situation.

The girls sat there. The server took their plates, refilled their coffee, and brought the check.

"Did Jackson answer your text? Hey, our flight is getting ready to board! Where the hell did they go?" Allison asked said in a panic.

Jan was feeling uneasy. She looked at the phone, the check, and the untouched food.

"We've got to get to the gate!" Allison said, standing up. "We've been here for two hours!"

"I know! Well, I'll just pay, and we'll go. I guess Jackson found somewhere else to eat. Damn! Jackson is such a flirt! Serves him right if he misses the flight! He's probably in some bar," Jan said as she paid the server for the food.

"Do you want to take this with you?" the server asked.

"No! Just toss it!" Jan snapped.

"They're calling us by name, Jan! We've got to get to the gate!" Allison yelled. "I bet they're waiting there for us."

They ran, rolling their luggage as quickly as they could, and arrived at their gate. They rushed to the counter.

"Can you tell me if Jackson and Brandon Taylor have boarded?" Jan asked, trying to catch her breath.

The flight attendant answered, "No, your parties have not boarded. Ladies, I need your tickets. This is the final boarding call."

Jan and Allison were numb. They looked at each other and then looked back at the flight attendant. The chairs in the seating area were empty.

"We can't board the plane without them. What if Brandon is sick?" Allison asked.

"Damn!" Jan said under her breath. She directed her attention to the agent and said, "We're not going to board without our traveling companions. Can we just change flights?"

"If you do not plan to board this flight, you'll need to go to the information counter to change flights, miss," the flight attendant instructed. "The doors are closing. You have missed your flight."

Jan and Allison walked over to the seating area and flopped down into a couple of chairs.

"Well, what the hell? Jackson hasn't answered my text messages, and they didn't show up when their names were called to get to the gate! What the hell?" Jan said desperately.

Allison looked at her phone. No messages from Brandon. "I'm worried. This is so strange. We need to go look for them. Let's go to the men's room. Who knows? Maybe they're both sick," Allison said with a shaky voice.

Jan shook her head. "Jackson better be sick, or I'm gonna kill him!"

They walked to the first men's room closest to the Whiskey River Restaurant. As they stood at the door to the men's room, Jan saw the maintenance man and said, "Excuse me, sir. Could you help us? Could you check the bathroom for our friends? They could be sick, and we don't know if they're okay."

"Sure. What are their names?" he asked.

"Jackson and Brandon," Jan answered.

The maintenance man walked in the men's room and yelled both names. He looked in each bathroom stall. Each stall was vacant.

The maintenance man came back out and said, "Sorry, ma'am. There's no one in here. I suggest you go to the information counter and have your friends paged."

Jan broke out in a cold sweat. *Something's not right here*, she thought. She felt a cold chill down her spine. "Thank you," she answered.

"Jan, we need to go to the information counter. What if they don't show up? They've disappeared! They've vanished!" Allison screamed.

"No, they haven't vanished, Allison," Jan snapped. "Come on. Let's go to the information counter."

They hurried to the information counter and explained everything to the agent. The agent promptly called the Transportation Security Administration. By the time security arrived, Jan and Allison were in tears.

Repeated calls for Jackson and Brandon were announced for them to meet their party, but it was fruitless. Hours passed by.

"We're going to have to call the police, ladies," the TSA agent informed them. "We have searched the premises, and there's no sign they're in the airport. They've either left the airport, or they've just disappeared."

It was now late. There were fewer flights and fewer travelers, so there were vacant seats throughout the airport. Shocked, Jan and Allison walked back to their gate and sat alone where they should have boarded a plane to go home.

Jan looked at Allison and asked, "How does one just disappear in an airport? Vanish? How is it...that a person is just...gone before breakfast?"

Chapter 4

Six Months Later

Jan boarded the plane and made her way to her assigned window seat. She looked around the plane and thought, *Not as full as it sometimes is on a Thursday. I guess nothing much is going on this weekend.*

Over the past six months, Jan had frequently traveled round trip from the Tri-Cities Regional Airport to the Charlotte International Airport. Every week, she boarded the plane on a Thursday and returned either on Friday or Saturday. She would spend her days walking around the concourses, looking for something that would tell her how someone could just disappear. Camera footage had been viewed and reviewed but showed nothing. But each week, Jan would travel to Charlotte hoping and praying to either miraculously find Jackson and Brandon at the airport or some clue that would explain what had happened to them.

This visit was different. She was meeting with John Connors, the Head of Charlotte International Airport's security. He had called her the previous week and asked that she meet with him. She was hoping that he had something to tell her. She had met with him several times over the last few months, but he never had any news for her. So, she was excited that he had reached out to her now.

The flight to Charlotte was short, usually taking only thirty or forty minutes to get there from the Tri-Cities. A small aircraft for the trip was to be expected. On this flight, harsh weather was moving in, making the flight over the mountains bumpy. Jan was tightening her seat belt when she heard a man's deep voice from across the aisle. She looked his way.

The man asked, "Hey . . . wonder if we paid extra for all this extra excitement?"

"Well, I think I want a refund if we did. This is too much for me," Jan said with a smile.

The man laughed nervously. "I totally agree."

He was interrupted when the flight attendant announced that passengers should make sure their seat belts were buckled tightly. As soon as the flight attendant made her announcement, the pilot interjected, "Sorry for the bumpy ride, folks. Looks like we'll be moving out of this soon."

Within a few minutes, the turbulence ceased, and the rest of the flight was smooth. The plane landed, and the passengers deplaned. As Jan stepped inside the terminal, she heard someone say, "I hope that you have safe travels, miss."

It was the man from the plane.

"Thanks. You, too," Jan said hurriedly.

She was rushing down the hallway when someone on an electric cart pulled up beside her and called out her name. It was John.

"I came to get you, but you slipped by me," John said.

"Sorry. I guess I was in a hurry to meet you," Jan replied.

"Yes. Let's go over to the coffee shop here so we can have a cup of coffee and talk," John instructed.

Jan hopped into the cart, John wheeled it around, and within a few minutes they were sitting in the corner of the coffee shop.

Jan was anxious. She sensed that John had news for her. "John, tell me what's up?"

John glanced down at his coffee for a moment, then looked straight into her eyes. "Jan, I don't know how to tell you this, but the case is going to be closed."

Jan was shocked. "How do people just disappear? And no one looks for them? Closed? What do you mean?" she asked, nearing a breaking point with tears in her eyes.

"Well, not exactly closed. The FBI will continue to keep the case open, but here at the airport, the case is no longer in our hands. I've been instructed not to spend any more time on this. I am so deeply sorry," John said.

"So, you can't help me anymore?" Jan asked.

"No. The FBI will be investigating totally. You *have* talked to them, right?" John asked.

"Yes," Jan answered, "but they don't tell me anything. It's always about asking me questions, and not me asking them questions. They have no answers for me. They wanted Jackson's computer and phone, but they disappeared when he did. He had them with him. They even searched his office. They keep calling and asking for information that I don't have."

"Maybe . . . maybe you should hire yourself an investigator," John suggested. "I swear. It's just like the brothers vanished into thin air. I don't have any clues. No film footage with them in it. Just nothing. I have nothing."

"What did the FBI tell you?" Jan asked. "And what did you tell the FBI?"

"Nothing much. They just told me and the police department that they are taking over this investigation, and if they need our help, they'll reach out to us. Do you think . . . well . . . I mean . . . is there a possibly that the brothers were part of . . . or working with . . . the cartel?"

Jan choked on her coffee as she spit out the words, "What!? What do you mean?"

"Well, the FBI looks in that direction for unsolved cases. And none of this makes sense. I mean—"

Jan interrupted, saying, "John, there's no way that Jackson and Brandon were involved with drugs. No way! Is that what the FBI is saying?"

"They're watching you, Jan. I am not supposed to tell you this. They think that you know what happened. So, like I said, you should get a private investigator. And maybe an attorney for your protection," John said quietly.

No words were spoken, just silence as John stood to leave. "I'm so very sorry," John said. "Something, I believe, happened to them. I don't think that they walked out of this airport. I just can't help you."

"Thank you for everything, John," Jan said, choking back tears.

John walked out of the coffee shop, hopped into the cart, and drove away. Jan sat there, staring into her cup of coffee.

I guess Allison is right. I'm going to have to put this behind me, Jan thought. *I've got to accept that Jackson is ...gone. For whatever reason, he is gone.*

Jan walked back to her gate. Her scheduled flight was the next day, but what was the point? She asked the agent to change her flight and to be put on standby for the next return flight later that day. She sat down in an empty waiting area and hid her face in tears. Minutes turned to hours. *How could this be?* she thought.

She was startled when she heard her name being announced. She walked to the counter.

"Ma'am, we have a seat for you."

"Thank you. My plans changed, so yes, I'm ready to go," Jan said.

Jan boarded the plane and took her seat. Pleasantly surprised, it was a window seat, and she was relieved that she could look out the window. Without looking up, a person sat next to her. She didn't look their way until the flight attendant stopped and said, "Ma'am, please fasten your seat belt."

"Oh, I'm sorry. Yes," Jan answered.

"Well, we meet again," said the person sitting next to her.

Jan looked, and to her surprise it was the gentleman from the earlier flight.

"Oh," she said, looking at him in amazement. "Small world."

"Yes. I guess it was quick business for you?" the stranger asked.

"Well, my plans changed. You?" Jan asked.

"Actually, yes. I get here and my appointment was canceled without notice. So, I just decided to head back, and by the way, my name is Lambert Holmes."

"Nice to meet you," Jan answered, "and I'm Jan Foster."

"My pleasure," Lambert replied. "So, you travel this route often? I think that I've seen you on this flight a few times."

"I've had personal things to attend to that required me to fly to Charlotte often, but…my business seems to have finished, I think," Jan said sadly.

"I hope all ended well," Lambert replied.

"Well, all about the same, actually," Jan said.

The pilot breaks their conversation with a joyful announcement. "Welcome and thank you for flying with us today. Our flight into the Tri-Cities Regional Airport is a short thirty-eight minutes and we hope that you enjoy your flight. We are third in line for takeoff and should be taking off shortly. Sit back, relax, and we will have you at your destination soon."

Jan looked out the window again. She didn't want to make small talk. She wanted to be left alone with her thoughts. But her thoughts were interrupted when Lambert asked, "Do you remember the flight down here? I sure hope we don't have that bumpy ride again."

Jan smiled but didn't reply.

"I take this flight often, and that was some of the worst turbulence I've been in on this route. Guess it was the bad weather. Are you from the Tri-Cities area? You and your husband?" Lambert asked.

Jan thought, *He isn't going to shut up.*

"Yes. Just me. You?" she asked.

"Well, I do travel around a lot, but the Appalachian Mountains are my home. With my work, I'm required to travel around, and no woman would like my work schedule, so there's no Mrs.," Lambert answered.

Jan didn't respond. She really didn't want to talk. The plane lifted into the air, and she thought, *I will be home soon…home…*

Lambert sat quietly for the rest of the flight, but as the plane touched down, he said, "Jan, if you might want to get a bite to eat sometime, there are a lot of good restaurants around here."

"But I thought you traveled a lot," Jan answered sarcastically.

They exited the plane, and inside the terminal Lambert called out to her, "Jan, here's my card. It's got my phone number on it, so call me. Let's have lunch or dinner sometime."

Lambert hands his card to her slowly. "Call me."

Jan took his card, smiled, and dropped the card into her handbag, then rushed to the bathroom. *Surely, he won't follow me in here*, she thought.

Chapter 5

The summer season was in full swing, and August weather was hot. Jan sat at her desk, staring at her computer, still numb from her last trip to Charlotte. *Should I go back this week as I've done for the last few months?* she asked herself.

She picked up her cell phone and called Allison.

Allison answered, "Hey, how are ya doing?"

"Allison, are you free for lunch today?" Jan quickly asked.

"Jan, if you're going to try to get me to go with you to Charlotte, the answer is still no," Allison said firmly.

"I really do need someone to talk to, Allison. I would rather talk to you than to Jackson's sister, Lisa. I have some distributing news," Jan said.

"What do you mean? Does someone know what happened?" Allison quickly asked.

"Let's do lunch. I can you meet you at The Peppermill Restaurant in Abingdon around eleven-thirty. Okay?" Jan asked.

Allison didn't immediately answer Jan. There was a moment of silence, and then she said, "Let's make it one. I'll see ya then." She hung up before Jan could confirm.

Jan was happy that Allison had finally agreed to meet with her. Allison had completely withdrawn from her after Jackson and Brandon disappeared. The last thing Allison had said to Jan was that she needed to get on with her life. Their last conversation was still fresh in Jan's memory.

"You need to move on, Jan, like I have. Jackson and Brandon either died or walked out of that airport, but either way, they left us. To me, they both died that day," Allison had said.

Jan's thoughts made her more anxious about meeting with Allison.

* * *

At 1:00 p.m., most of the lunch crowd was leaving, and the restaurant was not crowded. The warm weather was inviting to dine on the outdoor porch area. Jan arrived before Allison and Jan requested to be seated at a table for two on the porch.

"Do you want to wait for your guest to join you before you order?" the server asked. "Would you like to order a drink while you wait?"

"Yes, I'll wait until she arrives to order lunch, but I will go ahead and order a glass of your house red."

"Perfect. I'll be right back," the server said before walking away.

Jan sat and watched customers leave the restaurant. Everyone seemed to have a place to go and someone to go with them. She was lost in thought when her ringing cell phone broke the silence.

"Hello, Allison. Where are you?"

"I'm on my way. Sorry. There's a fender bender, and traffic is backed up. I just wanted to let you know that I am on my way," Allison said.

"Great. I've almost finished my first glass of wine and thought I'd have to start on my second one without you," Jan said teasingly.

"Nope. Wait for me! I'm on my way!" Allison said with a laugh.

Within a few minutes, Allison arrived and found the perfect parking spot along the street in front of the restaurant. She quickly spotted Jan sitting on the porch and walked directly to the table.

"Don't you love this weather? So glad that you got us a table out here," Allison said.

The server followed Allison to the table and asked, "Do you ladies need a few minutes?"

"Yes," Allison answered, "but I will have a glass of your best Sauvignon Blanc."

"You got it!" the server said.

"I like a gal who knows what she wants," Jan said with a smile. "And you look great! It's so good to see you!"

"It has been a while, hasn't it?" Allison said sheepishly as she sat down.

"Yes. It has. Why is that?" Jan asked.

"Here's your Sauvignon Blanc," the server announced. "Are you ladies ready to order?"

"Yes. I'm going to have my usual. The chicken lettuce wraps," Allison said.

"That works for me," Jan added.

Allison raised her glass to make a toast. "To best friends, always."

Jan smiled and raised her glass. "Always!"

When Allison finished a sip, she asked, "So, tell me, Jan, what's the latest?"

"Do you really want to know?" Jan asked.

"Yes and no," Allison replied. "And I do have something that I want to tell you."

"Tell me?" Jan asked.

"Yes, but you tell me first," Allison instructed.

"Well, my trip to Charlotte last week was probably my last trip. They're closing their investigation, and it's being turned over to the FBI," Jan said.

"The FBI has been investigating it from day one. So that doesn't surprise me," Allison replied.

"Why? Don't you find it odd that the FBI would be so interested in two men disappearing . . . from the airport?" Jan asked.

Allison didn't answer. She just stared at her.

"What is it that you haven't told me, Allison?" Jan asked.

"Well, the FBI has been asking you questions and asking me questions, so I think it's obvious that they think there's more to the story.

Don't you agree?" Allison asked. "They were in the airport, and poof! They were gone."

"You know something, don't you?" Jan asked.

"Jan, I don't know any more than you do. It's been tough on me for the last few months. Having to shut down the business. The FBI wanting to see our financials and going through everything. Not to mention putting me in the unemployment line. Closing the business, cleaning out the office, letting workers go, it's been heartbreaking. But I just couldn't keep it going," Allison said.

"And those life insurance policies they said they'd left us can't be touched until they are officially declared dead," Allison said coldly.

"Yes. I knew that Jackson always said that I would be taken care of if something were to happen to him," Jan said. "But he's not dead."

"Not officially," Allison responded. "And it'll be seven years of waiting and seeing. Not me. But . . . I found something that I guess I should've told you about before now," Allison said.

"Found something?" Jan asked. "What did you find?"

"I found the insurance policies when I was cleaning out the office safe. The life insurance policies are through Sentinel Mutual Insurance, and they're for two million dollars . . . each. Two million for you, and two million for me. And that's not all. There was a small amount of cash that Brandon always kept in the safe. But in the very back of the safe under the cash and papers, I found a black bag hidden. Inside the bag was three hundred thousand dollars cash and a note," Allison slowly said. "I'm sure it wasn't there before we left for St. Thomas. I would've seen it."

"I don't understand," Jan said.

"The note was wrapped around the money," Allison said. "Here's the note."

Jan took it and read.

My lovely Allison,
If you are reading this, then it's time for you to start a new life. Take the money and know that you deserve it and much more.
Love never ends,
Brandon

Jan handed the note back to Allison.

Interrupted by the server, "Here are your lunches, ladies. Would either like another glass of wine?"

"Yes!" both Jan and Allison answered simultaneously.

The server laughed and said, "I guess that was a yes!"

Jan and Allison said nothing as they started eating their lunches. Their wine was brought to the table, and the silence was broken when the server asked, "Is your food okay, ladies?"

Jan nodded yes, and Allison answered, "Perfect, thank you."

"Allison, I don't understand," Jan said.

"I don't know, either, Jan, but Brandon must have known that there was a possibly that he or Jackson—or both—was in some kind of trouble. And now the FBI is all over us, wanting more and more information that you and I don't have. Well, I'm done with it. I didn't tell the FBI about the money or the note, and I'm not going to. You can't tell them, either Jan. It won't help in any way," Allison said. "Either Brandon put that money in the safe right before we left for the trip, or someone put it there for him. Either way, it was from Brandon. And someone put those insurance policies in there, too."

"You don't think that telling the FBI about the money will help them find out what happened to them?" Jan asked.

"No, and at this point, do you really want to know?" Allison asked. "I don't. I loved Brandon, but like his note said, 'start a new life', and that's exactly what I'm doing. And it doesn't include him. Jan, are you trying to find out what happened to Jackson, or are you trying to find him? Both men made choices, and those choices obviously didn't include us. Jackson is gone, and do you really want to know what might have happened to him? You can't resurrect the dead or live with a ghost."

Jan choked back tears. Allison was right. If Jackson and Brandon had been in trouble and came to a tragic end, she didn't want to know the ugly details. *What if I found out that Jackson had been brutally murdered? What if he just up and left me for another woman? I wouldn't want to know that, either. So, am I trying to resurrect the living dead?* she thought.

"Think about it. If Jackson is alive, he has made no attempt to reach out to you," Allison said. "Same goes for Brandon. He has made no attempt to reach out to me. And finding that money . . . and those insurance policies, and that note . . . he's gone and doesn't intend to ever come back, dead or alive. And Jackson doesn't, either."

"I don't know how to get past this. I love Jackson. He is, or was, my everything," Jan said through tears.

"I'm done with it," Allison said. "I can get your insurance policy to you. And, I turned my policy over to the company's attorney, Robert Caudill. I had to reach out to him during the dissolving of the business, so I just gave the policy to him, too."

"You should have more questions than I do after finding that money. That's a lot of money. Where did that money come from?" Jan asked.

"I don't want answers," Allison said.

"Did you know that the FBI is watching me . . . or us?" Jan asked. "That's what John from the TSA told me last week."

"I guess that explains why I sometimes feel like someone's following me," Allison said. "But they won't find anything because I've got nothing to give them. And you . . . you need to start living again, Jan, and not by getting on an airplane to Charlotte every week, chasing a yesterday. The FBI has probably followed you on every trip you've made."

The server approached, interrupting. "Ladies, may I take your plates? And how are we doing on the wine?"

"Yes. We are finished here. No dessert, but check back on the wine later," Allison said with a wink.

"Will do," the server replied before walking away.

"I don't plan to stop looking and asking questions," Jan said bravely.

"I understand, Jan. But you'll have to do it without me. I'm done," Allison said sadly. "Have you talked to their sister, Lisa, lately?"

"No," Jan replied.

"Talk to her. Maybe she'll support you in looking for them. But I just can't," Allison said and changed the course of the conversation. "It does seem that Lisa stays busy with her travel agency. After her divorce, she's done well with the agency and seems pretty happy."

"Yes. She called me a couple of weeks ago and wanted me to go on this 'singles' scuba diving trip that is set over the holidays outside Belize. It's a private island, and the trip is by invitation only. Pretty expensive, but it sounded really nice. Are you doing any diving trips?" Jan asked.

"No. That was Brandon's thing, not mine. I know that you and Jackson loved that part of our trips, but I just went along for the vacation…the fun in the sun, not for the diving," Allison said with a smile. "You should consider taking her up on the invitation, Jan."

"I'm not sure that I can do that," Jan replied. "The holidays aren't going to be easy."

"And that's even more reason that you should go," Allison said.

The server approached their table again. "Ladies, another glass of wine?"

"No, I've got to get going. Just bring me the check," Allison instructed.

"Thanks, but you don't have to do that," Jan said. "Here's my faithful American Express."

"Hey, it's my treat. Let's say that it's on Brandon. Our way of saying goodbye to him," Allison said harshly.

"You really mean it, don't you, Allison?" Jan asked.

"Yes. I'm moving on," Allison said.

Chapter 6

The next day, Jan stayed busy at work, and it kept her mind off things. It was late afternoon when she found an old airline ticket stub in her desk drawer, and she started to cry. This was the first week since Jackson's disappearance that she wasn't hopping on a plane and going to Charlotte, hoping to find clues about what had happened. Her thoughts were interrupted when her cell phone rang.

"Hello, this is Jan," she answered, trying to gain her composure.

"Hi, Ms. Foster. This is Julia with American Express. I am calling you today to report that your American Express card was found at The Peppermill Restaurant in Abingdon, Virginia. Were you aware that your card was missing?"

"No," Jan answered. She grabbed her handbag and looked in her wallet. Her card was not there. "I must have dropped it yesterday when I had lunch there."

"The restaurant has offered to mail the card to us," Julia said.

"Thank you, but no. That won't be necessary. I can just run by the restaurant later and get it," Jan said.

"Perfect. So, you do not think that your card was stolen or compromised?" Julia asked.

"No, I must've dropped it. I will run by and pick it up. Thank you for calling me," Jan said.

"Thank you. We appreciate your business. Have a wonderful day," Julia said and ended the phone call.

Jan looked at her watch and thought, *Almost 3:30 p.m. I will go now and pick it up before the dinner crowd shows up.*

When Jan arrived at the restaurant, there was a loud boom. Raindrops gently splashed on her windshield. She parked, grabbed her umbrella, and walked swiftly inside.

"Welcome. I believe it's coming a storm out there," the greeter said. "Will you be dining with us this evening?"

"Actually, I'm Jan Foster, and evidently I dropped my American Express card here yesterday and was told that I could pick it up," Jan said.

"Oh yes, Ms. Foster. We didn't have a phone number for you, so we called American Express, and they told us that they would reach out to you," the greeter said. "Let me get it for you."

Jan looked outside, and it was pouring rain.

"Here's your card. Do you really want to go out there right now?" the greeter asked upon returning.

"Thank you. You know, I think that I'll have a glass of wine in the bar and just wait for a while," Jan said with a smile.

"I don't blame you," the greeter replied.

Jan made her way to the bar and sat at a high-top table near a window. She ordered a glass of wine and watched a couple of people run to the restaurant's door through the pouring rain. She glanced at her watch and thought, *I don't want to be here alone with couples coming in for dinner.* She looked back out the window.

"Well, what a coincidence!" a man said loudly, walking toward her table. "I can't believe we keep running into each other."

This cannot be happening, she thought. It was Lambert Holmes.

"Isn't this great weather for ducks?" Lambert asked as he, uninvited, sat down in the empty chair at her table.

"Yes, what a coincidence! We do seem to keep running into each other," Jan said, trying to be polite.

"Are you dining alone this evening?" Lambert asked.

"No, not exactly," Jan answered. "I . . . I . . . just stopped by to . . . to get out of the rain."

"Well, there's not a better way to do that," Lambert laughed. "Just stop in and have a glass of wine."

Jan was afraid to ask him if he was dining alone or meeting someone. *What if I am stuck with him all evening? I've got to finish this wine and get out of here*, she thought.

"Hey, what a treat for me! I see my two most favorite people in the world have already met each other," echoed a voice from the doorway. Walking into the bar was Allison smiling from ear to ear.

Allison walked over to Lambert and planted a kiss on his forehead. Jan was speechless.

"Well, I guess I don't need to do introductions, now do I?" Allison asked, grinning.

"Nope! I met your best friend on a flight a while back," Lambert boasted. "Grab a chair and scoop in here!"

Jan couldn't think of anything to say. However, the expression on her face said exactly what she was thinking. *How disgusting!*

"Jan, are you meeting someone here for dinner?" Allison asked enthusiastically.

"No. I accidentally dropped my American Express card here yesterday and stopped by to pick it up. I just got caught in the rain and decided to wait for the storm to pass," Jan answered cautiously.

"Well, don't dine alone. You have to join us for dinner," Allison said persuasively.

"No, I couldn't do that," Jan said. "I really need to get going, and the rain's letting up now."

"Nonsense! You gotta eat, don't ya?" Lambert asked. "We insist that you join us."

"We won't take no for an answer," Allison said. "Besides, Lambert might be the man you want to talk to."

"How so?" Jan asked coldly.

"Why, he's a private investigator," Allison said. "You didn't know that? Lambert, didn't you tell her?"

"Didn't have much of a chance. We made introductions and didn't speak much more than that," Lambert said.

He looked to Jan and asked, "So, you need an investigator?"

The server interrupted the conversation, saying, "Your table is ready."

"I'm going to leave and let the two of you enjoy your dinner," Jan quickly blurted out, standing up. "But some other time." She grabbed her purse and darted for the door.

"Hey, you forgot your umbrella," Lambert said, jumping up to hand it to her. As he handed Jan the umbrella, he leaned over her shoulder and whispered in a low voice, "Call me."

She bolted through the door, ran to her car, quickly opened the car door, and tossed her handbag over to the passenger's seat as she jumped inside. The handbag opened, spilling the contents everywhere. Jan gathered her things from the floor of the car and put them back into the handbag. She noticed a business card on the floor mat and picked it up. It read:

Lambert Holmes, Private Investigator
AT YOUR SERVICE
Discreet and Confidential
Call 555-LAM-BERT

Geez, he just won't go away, she thought.

Chapter 7

The next morning, Jan's phone rang at 7:00 a.m.. She normally slept in on Saturday mornings but had not been able to do that since Jackson's disappearance.

She looked at the caller ID. It was Allison.

"Good morning, Allison. How did you know that I'd be up at this hour on a Saturday?" Jan asked teasingly when she answered the phone.

"I just knew," Allison answered. "So, what did you think?"

"About what?" Jan asked.

"About what? About Lambert?" Allison asked. "What did you think about him?"

Jan hesitated. She wasn't sure what to say without sounding rude. "Well…the question is…what do you think?" she asked. "And how did you ever meet him?"

"How about you and I do some shopping and have lunch today. It's going to be a beautiful day, and we can talk all about it!" Allison replied excitedly.

"Sounds great! What do you have in mind?" Jan asked.

"If you are up for it, let's drive over to Blowing Rock. I will pick you up around ten, and we'll make it a day," Allison said.

Blowing Rock, North Carolina, was just a little over an hour-long drive from the Tri-Cities, and the scenery was never disappointing.

"Sure. That'll work. I'll be ready!" Jan answered.

* * *

Jan showered and dressed, and at precisely 10:00 a.m., Allison pulled into her driveway in her convertible BMW, the top down, honking the horn.

Jan stepped out the door, yelling, "I'm coming!"

The drive was refreshing. The ride in the convertible was perfect with the warm summer air. Jan and Allison talked about everything but Jackson and Lambert. The laughter and light conversation were delightful for both of them.

As they arrived on Main Street in Blowing Rock, Jan pointed, "Look, there's a parking spot. Just perfect and convenient to carry all our bargains."

Allison asked, "Great! Are you hungry?"

"Yes. I didn't have breakfast, just a cup of coffee," Jan answered.

"Well, let's eat at The Village Café, because I made reservations to be sure to get a table," Allison said. "We can do a lot more shopping with full stomachs."

They laughed and made their way from the car to the restaurant. They went down the steps to the restaurant and were quickly seated in the outdoor area. With the sun shining and the warm breeze, the outdoor seating was perfect. Service was quick, and they both ordered wine to drink and the lunch special of the day.

"Jackson and I used to come here often and stay at Chetola. And this was our favorite restaurant," Jan said sadly.

"Yes, Brandon liked coming here, too. Remember when all of us rented a condo and stayed here in July for the Symphony on the Lake? That was such a fun, magical weekend. But...things have changed, Jan," Allison said seriously.

"Yes, and more for you than me. So, tell me all about Lambert. How on earth did the two of you meet?" Jan asked.

It was hard for Allison to hide her excitement. "Actually, I've known him for a while. He dropped by the office a few times and was a friend of Brandon's. He would bring us referrals or someone for Brandon to contact for landscaping jobs. He often visited the office," Allison said smiling.

"And he knows about Jackson and Brandon?" Jan asked.

"Everyone knows, Jan. The whole world knows! So, yes. But Lambert came by when I was clearing out the office, selling off stuff, closing things down, and he was really a lot of comfort to me," Allison said defensively.

"Well, I just meant that it was a coincidence that he just happened to come around when Brandon disappeared, but obviously he knew you anyway," Jan said softly. "I guess he didn't understand what happened to them, either, and with his profession, he just wanted to help."

"Well, yes. He offered to investigate for me, but I told him no," Allison said. "Actually, after finding the money and the note, I knew that Brandon was gone."

"You didn't tell him about the money, did you?" Jan quickly asked.

"No. That's our secret," Allison replied. "Lambert seems to do more investigative work for personal things, like people skipping out on child support and things of that nature."

"Interesting that he's been on the same flights to Charlotte that I'm usually on," Jan said.

"He did have some investigative work in Charlotte. So did you see him?" Allison asked.

"Well, yes. The one time," Jan said. "But he said that he traveled there a lot. Why didn't you have him see what he could find out?"

"Well, after the FBI kept coming around, and after finding that money, I was simply afraid of what Lambert would discover," Allison answered.

"So, you trust him?" Jan asked.

"Yes," Allison answered.

"You like him, don't you?" Jan asked.

Allison's face turned a little red, and she giggled like a child and answered, "Yes. *And* I have slept with him. And yes, I do like him."

They both laughed.

"You think that I should hire him to investigate?" Jan asked.

"Well, if he's as good at investigating as he is in bed, absolutely!" Allison said proudly.

Jan laughed out loud.

"But really, Jan, I don't want him to be that involved. I mean, what would happen if he found Brandon? I mean I will always love Brandon, but now I'm involved with Lambert. What would I do?" asked Allison. "I think that Lambert and I should just see what happens with us. And I will always love Brandon, but he left me … clearly."

"Well, I guess things could get complicated," Jan said. "I guess I understand. Did you tell Lambert about the FBI following us?"

"Well, I told him that the FBI had questioned us but that we knew nothing. We simply don't know what happened to them. Lambert assured me that the FBI was just fishing and that they don't have a clue, either."

Their server walked over to the table and asked, "Ladies, another glass of wine?"

"Hey, let's do another! We have all day," Allison said.

"Works for me!" Jan said.

They each ordered another glass of wine, and the conversation changed from work to shopping. Jan was relieved that Allison didn't insist that she hire Lambert to investigate. She didn't trust Lambert but didn't want Allison to know. It was clear that Allison had fallen for him and was ready to move forward in her life without Brandon.

* * *

Jan and Allison spent the entire day shopping, eating, and enjoying the day together. They decided to have dinner and head back home.

When they arrived at Jan's house, Jan got out of the car and said, "It is almost nine. You want to come in and have a drink? Or you're welcome to stay over."

"I've really enjoyed today. I needed this. I think that we both did. But I'm going on home. I'm okay to drive. It's just another twenty minutes or so. And my phone is ringing off the hook. It's Lambert. I told him we would be back by eight. Guess he's wondering what happened to us," Allison said with a wink. "Thanks! Talk to ya soon!"

Allison pulled out of the driveway, and Jan went inside. She quickly showered and went to bed. She was tired, but as she drifted to sleep, she thought, *What a wonderful day!*

Chapter 8

Six Years Later

Six months turned into six years. Jan pushed herself into her work, and Allison's time was mostly spent with Lambert, and working part-time for a CPA firm. Nothing had developed in finding Jackson and Brandon, and the FBI had not asked questions for a couple of years. Jan had watched the anniversary date of Jackson's and Brandon's disappearance come and go for six years. Valentine's Day was always so hard because they had always spent Valentine's Day in St. Thomas. It had been magical. But Valentine's Day came and went now, and it was just another date on the calendar.

Snow was falling. The weather had been bad all day. Jan decided to leave work early because the snow was accumulating, and the weather forecast predicted that it would get worse. She pulled out of the parking lot and was getting onto the highway when her cell phone rang. It was Allison.

"Jan?" Allison asked in a weak voice when Jan answered.

"Hey, how are you? I haven't talked to you in a while. How're things going?" Jan asked.

There was a long pause. "Jan…" Allison said before bursting into tears.

"Allison, what's wrong?" Jan asked.

There was a long silence. Through her tears, Allison said brokenly, "I need to see you."

"Of course. I was headed home, but I'll turn around right now and will be at your place in a few minutes," Jan answered. "What's wrong?"

Click. Allison ended the call.

Jan made a quick U-turn and headed to Allison's place. *What could possibly be wrong?* she thought. *Could it be about Jackson and Brandon?*

Jan drove cautiously on the slippery roads and managed to speed through a couple of red lights and arrived quickly. She got out of her car, ran to the door, and rang the doorbell.

"Come on in," Allison yelled.

When Jan walked inside, she was shocked to see that Allison was a mess. Her eyes were swollen, and she appeared very distraught.

"My stars! Allison, what in the world is wrong?" Jan asked.

Allison was almost inconsolable.

"He was killed in a car accident!" she cried. "My Lambert's gone. He died!"

Jan stood frozen. She felt guilty for hoping it was about Jackson and Brandon, and she felt so sorry for Allison. It was clear that Allison was in love with Lambert.

"Oh, Allison. I am so deeply sorry," she said. "How did you find out? Who told you? I mean, what happened?"

Allison composed herself and poured herself another glass of wine. "Grab a glass from the kitchen," she instructed Jan.

Jan grabbed a glass from the kitchen, came back, and poured herself a glass of wine. "Tell me, Allison," she said. "What happened?"

Allison struggled to keep it together. "I know that you didn't care much for Lambert, but he really was a good guy with a good heart," she said. "We were in love. It just happened between us. It just seemed right."

"Tell me what happened," Jan said.

"Well, he had been on some investigation and was coming home and hit some black ice on the road, according to his sister, he lost control of the car, and his car crossed the highway into the path of a tractor and trailer…" Allison said and couldn't say anything more for crying.

"Oh, Allison, how sad! I am so sorry!" Jan said. She hugged Allison, and they cried together.

The wine was soothing to Allison and it helped calm her. "Jan, do you know what this past week was?" Allison asked.

"Yes. It's been six years," Jan answered cautiously.

"I feel like I'm cursed," Allison said.

"No. You're not cursed. Think about it. You've had an opportunity to feel love again. You had love with Brandon, and then you had love with Lambert. That's pretty special," Jan said, hoping that her resentment didn't show. She resented that Allison could so easily forget about Brandon and move on with someone new, and Allison was more upset over losing Lambert than Brandon.

"I did love Lambert. He was caring, sensitive, and so willing to do whatever to make me happy," Allison said. "He wasn't Brandon, but he made me laugh. He made me happy."

Jan tried to be sympathetic even though it was not easy. She didn't like Lambert. She'd never trusted him. Maybe his line of work made her feel like he wasn't truthful.

"So, you talked to his sister?" Jan asked without being too specific.

"Yes. His sister, Elaine, was the one who called me. She lives in Richmond, Virginia, and said that she would fly down tomorrow to help take care of things. He was taken to the Abingdon Funeral Home. He and I…not being married…I can't make any decisions," Allison said. "And besides, he and I never discussed the what ifs in life. We talked about a future and maybe moving in together, but we never really talked about…death."

"Lambert was divorced. Did he have children?" Jan asked.

"No. He got divorced several years ago and had no children. I think it was just him and his sister. She's the next of kin. His parents are deceased," Allison said.

"Elaine would be considered closest family, which is best," Jan said. "For now, you need to try to get some rest, Allison. We'll have a long week of preparation. We'll need to pick up Elaine at the airport, and she'll need our help. You know I'm here for you. I'm so sorry, Allison."

"Thank you. I really appreciate you. You're my best friend. And you're right. I'm just in shock. How could this be?" Allison asked. "We just had a wonderful Valentine's Day dinner a few nights ago. And now . . . he's gone." She broke down in tears.

* * *

The next few days moved quickly. Allison and Jan picked up Elaine at the airport and gave her a quick tour of the area. So much had changed since she'd lived there. She insisted that she stay at Lambert's condo, and she quickly put things into motion. The services for Lambert were held on a Thursday at the Abingdon Memorial, and his ashes were placed in a vault after the service. Allison and Jan had helped contact friends and acquaintances. The service was small and private.

"I think that he would have been very pleased with all this," Elaine said as she, Allison, and Jan made their way to the car after the service.

"Yes," Allison agreed.

"Even though a small gathering, Lambert did seem to have a lot of friends," Jan added. Jan hesitated but asked, "Would either one of you want to get a bite to eat? We can go to The Peppermill Restaurant."

"Yes," Allison answered quickly. "That was our favorite restaurant. Lambert would appreciate us spending time there in his remembrance. A celebration of his life."

"Sounds good," Elaine said.

* * *

At the restaurant, the three of them talked about Lambert. Jan was entertained by the 'he said, or he did' conversations between Elaine and Allison. It seemed to help Allison to talk about Lambert, memories and recalling their laughter together.

Elaine finally changed the course of the conversation. "I've been packing up Lambert's things, and movers are supposed to pick up everything on Monday. There are personal things that I'm sure you'll want, Allison. Can you help me finish up this weekend?"

Allison seemed surprised by the bluntness but answered, "Yes. Definitely."

"I've boxed up his clothes, dishes, and furniture to give away, so if there's anything you want, feel free to take it," Elaine said. "He lived like a minimalist."

"He lived like most men," Allison said. "But he did like auctions, and antiques, so there are a few things I'll take and keep. His desk is one of them."

"Certainly," Elaine said. "But we have to have everything out by Monday evening. The landlord is ready to rent the condo, and I'm flying out on Tuesday since I have to be back at work on Wednesday. Also, Lambert's safe has to be moved. It's small, but it's heavy, and I can't find the combination."

"His safe?" Jan asked quickly.

"Yes. He kept confidential papers in there," Allison replied. "I don't have the combination, but I guess I should take the safe. We don't know what might be in it."

"When the movers come on Monday, you should probably ask if they can drop it and the desk off at your place. It would be easier," Elaine said. "And the rest of the stuff is going to be donated to Goodwill."

"What do you think is in the safe?" Jan asked inquisitively.

"Just personal stuff and confidential stuff about his investigations," Allison answered. "He used to tell me that his career secrets were in that safe and that they were safe and sound, and then he would laugh."

"Well, it just makes sense that you should take it, but I'm not sure how you're going to get it open," Elaine said.

"I don't guess there's any hurry," Allison said sadly. "But I'll take it, his desk, and any pictures of us."

* * *

Allison and Elaine worked together at the condo, packing up Lambert's things and cleaning out the condo. Jan helped as much as she could, but she was being pushed with deadlines at work. On Monday afternoon, she took a break and called Allison.

"Hey, how are you doing?" Jan asked.

"Okay, I guess. Movers just left. They dropped off the desk and safe," Allison said through tears.

"Where's Elaine?" Jan asked.

"I loaned her my car so she could follow the movers, and then she's going to stay here tonight. She has an early flight in the morning. I'm going to take her to the airport," Allison said.

"Do you need me to come over?" Jan asked.

"Not really. I know that you have been busy with work. I'm just going to take a hot bath and go to bed. I'm exhausted, and I'm sure Elaine is, as well. I'll call you when I've dropped her off at the airport. Maybe we can do lunch," Allison suggested.

"Sounds like a plan. Just call me if you need anything before," Jan said.

Chapter 9

The days turned into weeks, and the weeks turned into months. Jan and Allison got together as often as they could. Spring turned into summer, and the Fourth of July celebration was now coming up over the weekend. The holiday would fall on Saturday, so many businesses would be closed on Friday for the celebration. Allison was busy working part-time at a small accounting firm, but she wouldn't be working on Friday. Jan stayed busy meeting deadlines and signing new publishing contracts, but she decided that she, too, would take Friday off from work and stay clear of her computer.

On Thursday evening, Jan's phone rang. "What? It is seven! Another telemarketer?" she said out loud to herself before she looked at the caller ID. But it was Jackson's sister, Lisa. *Hmm, it's been a while since I have heard from her,* she thought as she answered the phone.

"This is Jan," she answered.

"Hey, Miss Jan, this is Lisa. How are you doing? Is now a good time to talk?" Lisa said hurriedly.

"Sure. It's good to hear from you! How are you doing?" Jan asked.

"Good! Staying busy making vacation plans and helping get travel groups together. Which brings me to why I'm calling. I would like to invite you over to my house for a presentation on this new resort in Belize. It's fabulous. You can only visit if you're invited, and through my travel agency I have received an invitation. I can bring a limited number of guests. This is the resort that has been growing over the last few years, and I mentioned it a while back. Would love for you to consider it," Lisa said.

"I would love to see you, but I'm not really doing any traveling," Jan said.

"Do you still go scuba diving?" Lisa asked slowly.

Jan hesitated but answered, "I haven't been since Jackson and Brandon disappeared."

There was a short silence, then Lisa kindly said, "I know that they're missed."

"I guess the investigation ended," Jan said. "This coming February will be seven years, and I haven't heard from any FBI agents in a long time."

"Me, either," Lisa said. "It was really hard to lose both brothers at the same time. I try not to think about it, so I stay on the road traveling as much as I possibly can, and that's why I'm planning this boutique trip. Please come over. I've asked Allison, but I'm not sure she'll attend. She might if you do."

"Well, I would love to see you. I'll give Allison a call, and see if she'll come with me," Jan said.

"Great! Saturday. At sixish, we'll eat—I'm having it catered; it will be buffet style—and then we'll watch the presentation. Then we'll watch fireworks from the deck. You know they set off the best fireworks here at the lake, and from my deck I have a great view," Lisa said proudly.

"Oh yes! Being on the lake, you have a great view year-round," Jan said sweetly. "I'll plan on it."

After hanging up, Jan decided to call Allison the next day. She wanted to give the invitation some thought. She showered and went to bed early. As she drifted off to sleep, her thoughts kept bouncing around in her head. *How could I think about a vacation? I'm not sure that I can ever go on a scuba diving trip again*, she thought. *Do I really want to consider this?*

* * *

The next morning, Jan was awakened by her phone ringing.

"Did I wake you?" Allison asked.

"Sort of, I guess," Jan replied. "I decided to take today off from work. I just need a break."

"Good for you! I have the day off, too. Let's go to the lake, rent a boat, and sunbathe all day," Allison suggested.

"That sounds like fun! How will we get a boat?" Jan asked.

"I will call right now, and be on my way," Allison said.

Click. She'd hung up.

Jan hopped out of bed, showered, and dressed for a lake day. She was finishing her packing, when she heard the doorbell ring.

She opened the door, and Allison asked, "Are you ready?"

"Yes. Were you able to rent a boat?" Jan asked.

"Yes! And it's a large one. We'll even have a captain and crew. They'll be taking us out for the day on this cruiser," Allison said excitedly.

"On South Holston Lake? We'll have a cruiser and crew? Are you sure?" Jan asked, confused.

"Yes! I have a client who owns a cruiser. He rents it out for the day with his own crew, so he doesn't have to worry about a novice destroying it out on the lake. He offered. And why not? We'll have it until about six. There's a kitchen, and the food is prepared. This'll feel like we are in the big league of cruising. It'll be like we are on a yacht! All on SOHO!" Allison said with a giggle.

"This, I gotta see!" Jan yelled.

* * *

Jan and Allison arrived at the Sportsman's Marina to find that the cruiser exceeded all expectations. It was refurbished and had been designed in exquisite detail. They met the captain, the first mate, and a female chef.

"Ladies, we're here to serve. And we want to make your day enjoyable," the captain announced. "I'm Captain Jack."

Captain Jack gave them a tour of the cruiser and handed them a daily agenda that noted their stopping points on the lake, the midmorning snack that would be served, the lunch they would have, and the midafternoon snack they would be given. There was also a list of available beverages, including cocktails.

After Jan and Allison had changed into their bathing suits and settled into their chairs with their umbrella drinks, Jan asked, "I don't mean to sound unappreciative, but this has to be expensive. How much is this costing us?"

"Actually, it is a little pricey," Allison whispered. "It starts at twelve hundred dollars, and the price goes up depending on the number of people and so on. But our cost? We're getting this for free."

"Free?" Jan screamed.

"Hush!" Allison instructed.

"Oops!" Jan murmured.

"He's a new client, and I worked on his taxes. He's been overpaying, so I was able to get him a big tax refund. He was so grateful that he offered this as a way to say thank you for great service," Allison said proudly. "I have to be careful what I say, or it might look like a bribe." She winked.

"So, this is legit?" Jan asked.

"Totally," Allison answered.

The day was fabulous. There were very few clouds in the sky, with a warm breeze. There were a lot of boaters on the lake, but the ladies didn't mind all the stares and waves from passing boaters.

After lunch, Jan and Allison were sipping their third cocktail when Jan broke the silence. "I talked to Lisa yesterday, and she said that she called you about her trip presentation at her house tomorrow night. Do you want to go?"

Allison looked at her and replied, "Maybe if you're going. *Are* you going?"

"I don't think that I'll seriously consider the trip, but I would like to see Lisa. She's always either on the ocean or in the sky. Always traveling. But to consider another scuba diving trip…well, I'm just not sure. And I didn't ask her if it was for singles or couples," Jan said.

"I just took it that it was for singles. But you know that I don't scuba dive, so I'm not sure why she would even ask me," Allison said.

"Maybe it's just an opportunity for us to get together. It was nice that she asked," Jan said.

"Maybe. So, do you want to go?" Allison asked. "I hope that it's not a singles evening meant to fix us up with someone."

Jan was a little surprised. "I never really thought of that, but I don't think so. So, let's go. I'll come by around five-thirty and pick ya up. We'll get to see free fireworks on the lake," she said with a snicker.

They both laughed at the thought of being at the lake…again.

Chapter 10

Allison and Jan arrived at Lisa's house at 5:45 p.m.

"Wow! Look at this house! A mansion on the lake!" Allison announced as Jan parked her car on the side of the street.

"And look at all these cars! She must have invited everyone in the county," Jan said.

"Are you sure you want to do this?" Allison asked.

"Got to now. Look who's running down the driveway," Jan said under her breath, pointing.

"Girls, perfect timing! So glad ya both came. It's going to be fun," Lisa said with excitement. "And of course, you're under no obligation to go on the trip, but wait until you see this resort. You'll love this place!"

Lisa directed Allison and Jan walk through the front door, and made their way to the outside deck, which was as large as a ballroom. The partially covered deck area had lots of seating, a small fireplace, and an abundance of food and wine.

"Grab a glass of wine or whatever, get some food, mingle, and grab a seat," Lisa said with a wink. "I'm going to start this show shortly."

The food had been catered by the best caterer available, and a bartender poured endless drinks into seemingly bottomless glasses.

"Do you see anyone you know?" Jan asked as she grabbed a glass of wine and sipped.

"I see a few people who look familiar, but I can't say for sure," Allison answered. "How about you?"

"I do recognize two couples. See them over there?" Jan discreetly pointed. "They were always on our scuba trips."

"Oh yes. I guess so. They do look a little familiar, just older. But I guess we look older, too," Allison said. "And I do recognize Allen. He's the banker. Remember him? He lost his wife to cancer a few years ago."

Jan wasn't really listening to Allison. Her thoughts strayed to the scuba trips that she and Jackson had taken together. It was hard to believe that in a few months it would hit the seven-year mark, and there were still no clues about what had happened to Jackson and Brandon.

"Jan, did you hear me? We need to grab a seat," Allison repeated. "Lisa's about to get started."

"Oh, yes. Just daydreaming," Jan answered as they sat down in two vacant seats nearby.

"Ladies and gents, welcome! Thank you so much for being here this evening. Your being here tells me that you can't wait to find out about the newest and most impressive resort around. So, let's get started!"

Lisa started her presentation with handouts and a video that highlighted all of the perks of this one-of-a-kind resort. The presentation lasted about an hour, and the resort appeared to be magnificent.

"As we finish, let me remind you that this resort is on a private island off Belize, and it opened up completely to the public this year with limited reservations. The trip details are in your handouts. This trip is over Christmas and New Year's. The resort brings in local families on Christmas Eve, and of course, Santa Claus will have gifts for the children. And then on Christmas Day, the resort provides a huge dinner for locals and their guests. There will be private scuba lessons, fishing trips, diving excursions, midnight yacht sailings, snorkeling, and so much more. I can schedule arrival times on the day after Christmas or the day before Christmas Eve. What a beautiful way to spend the Christmas holiday! Please fill out the card in your packet and specify the dates you prefer. You'll have until July fifteenth for the discounts, but I need to confirm air travel for the holiday season now.

"Got questions? Let's schedule a time to talk. Enjoy the rest of your evening by joining me downstairs. The food and drinks have been moved there. We'll all have front-row seats to watch the magnificent fireworks, which will start momentarily. Thank you again!" Lisa said, finishing the presentation.

"Well, I'm ready for some fireworks, and another glass of wine," Allison said as she stood up.

"Sounds good to me," Jan agreed.

As they made their way downstairs, they heard people exchange comments about the trip and the resort. The mood was very upbeat. When they got downstairs, Allison walked over to the bartender, got a glass of wine for herself and one for Jan. Jan found two empty chairs for them and sat down.

Allison came over and handed a glass of wine to Jan. She sat down and asked, "Lisa did a wonderful job on the presentation, didn't she?"

"She sure did. And what a resort!" Jan answered.

"You should go," Allison said.

"Me? Why not you? Why not us?" Jan asked.

"I don't scuba dive, but you do. And Jan, you haven't done anything fun since Jackson disappeared. It's time you do," Allison said very seriously.

"I don't know," Jan answered. "During the holidays ... with families everywhere ... I'm just not sure. But that resort is quite special. You and I could both go. You don't have to scuba dive."

There was suddenly a loud boom. The fireworks started with a bang and lasted for over an hour. When the fireworks ended, and guests were leaving, Lisa made her way over to Jan and Allison.

"Hey, ladies, you can't leave without signing up to go," Lisa said with a big smile.

"Lisa, what a wonderful presentation! And how did you ever find this resort?" Jan said.

"You know me. I'm always looking for the best for less in traveling," Lisa answered.

"Is the place for real?" Allison asked.

"Sure is. I visited a few times before it went public, and it's all it claims to be and more," Lisa answered. "So, you're both going, aren't you?"

"Not me," Allison said. "But I think Jan should definitely do this."

"You both should! I'll call you Monday and work out the details," Lisa said before turning to another guest.

Later, while they were on their way home, Jan and Allison made small talk until Allison turned the conversation to the trip. "Jan, you really should go on this trip. Do it for you," she encouraged.

"Without you? But you're like me. We dread holidays since we have little to no family," Jan said.

"True. But you're closer to Lisa than I am, and she really wants you to go on this trip," Allison said.

"Well, let's think about it and give Lisa an answer on Monday," Jan said thoughtfully.

"Yes. Sounds good," Allison agreed.

* * *

On Monday morning, Jan's phone rang at 9:30 a.m. She saw it was Lisa and answered.

"Hey, I know it's early on a workday, but I wanted to get with you before your day started. Let's do lunch!" Lisa said.

"Okay. Where and when?" Jan asked.

"Our usual. The Peppermill. One o'clock. And bring Allison. See you there," Lisa said, then hung up.

Jan quickly called Allison.

"Hey," Allison answered.

"We're meeting Lisa at The Peppermill at one today," Jan said.

There was a hesitation, and then Allison said, "No. I'm not going. I thought about it, and this trip is not for me."

"But I don't want to go without you," Jan replied.

"Do it for you," Allison said.

"Are you sure?" Jan asked.

"Yes, I'm sure," Allison said, softness in her voice.

* * *

Jan and Lisa finished their lunch before Lisa started her sales pitch.

"Bring us each another glass of wine," Lisa instructed the server. "Okay, Jan, let's talk."

"I guess I've been avoiding this conversation," Jan said with a smile.

"I know that you wanted Allison to go with you on this trip, but you won't be the only single person there. There'll be others. And you can be *my* tagalong," Lisa said.

"You? Isn't…what's his name? Isn't Josh going with you?" Jan asked.

"Yes, Josh is his name, and no. He's going to be spending time with his family this holiday," Lisa said.

"What about New Year's Eve?" Jan asked sadly.

"There's going to be a 'singles' New Year's Eve party. I'll be there. So, no excuses. You have to go with me. You'll enjoy all the perks I do, because you'll be with me," Lisa said. "Besides, this resort is very private, and only a select number of guests are allowed to come."

"I just don't know—"

"It's done. Your airfare is paid for, your upgraded room is comped, and it's done!" Lisa announced, interrupting her.

"Well, how can I say 'no' to that?" Jan asked reluctantly.

"You can't," Lisa said quickly.

* * *

As Jan drove back to the office, she called Allison.

Allison answered her phone with a question: "Did you tell her that you'd go?"

"What do you think?" Jan teased.

"Yes?" Allison asked.

"Okay, I told her that I'd go. She offered me free airfare and a free upgraded room, and I just couldn't say no. She seemed so insistent," Jan answered.

"You're doing the right thing. It'll do you good," Allison said. "And if you are unhappy, you can always head back home."

"Well, that's true. I guess if I feel uncomfortable, I can just head back home," Jan said in agreement.

Chapter 11

Autumn brought beautiful, colorful leaves and a crispness in the air, but it quickly turned into the holiday season. December was here, and Jan was excited about her vacation. She had just finished packing her suitcase when her phone rang. It was Allison.

"Hey, are you packed yet? You leave tomorrow," Allison asked teasingly when Jan answered.

"You know me. I've been packed for months," Jan said, laughing. "But your timing is great. I did just finish. Bags are sitting at the door and ready to go. The bags are ready to go, but I'm not sure *I'm* ready to go, but Lisa is picking me up early in the morning."

"Well, why don't ya come over and help me decorate my Christmas tree, and we'll have an early dinner," Allison suggested.

"You put up a tree?" Jan asked.

"Sort of. This tree has been sitting in my living room for a week now, with just the lights glowing. Looks pretty at night, but it's sort of sad during the day," Allison said. "So, come on over. We'll order pizza."

"Perfect," Jan replied. "See ya shortly."

* * *

When Jan arrived at Allison's house, Allison opened the door before she could ring the doorbell.

"Hey, did you bring the snow with you?" Allison asked with a smile.

"It's only flurries," Jan answered.

"It's just the start of what is forecasted to come in here on Christmas Eve," Allison said as she shut the door. They walked into the living room. "Have you heard? We're supposed to have a foot of snow. Weather alerts are already being posted."

"No, I hadn't heard," Jan said, puzzled. "Guess I should be glad that I'm leaving tomorrow, the day before it hits. And here. Merry Christmas!" She handed Allison a bottle of wine.

"You know this is my favorite gift," Allison said, and they both laughed. "And Merry Christmas to you!" She handed a wrapped box to Jan.

"What's this?" Jan asked.

"Open it," Allison instructed. "But first, I'll open this wine." She went to the kitchen and came back with two glasses of wine. She handed one to Jan. "To best friends," she toasted.

"To best friends," Jan repeated.

Jan set down her glass and unwrapped her gift. She was overcome with emotion when she saw the hand-crafted Christmas ornament. On it was a picture of her and Allison, along with the words *Best Friends.* "This is so special! Thank you!" Jan said, tearful. "I love this and will always treasure it."

"You know, it's hard to buy for someone who has everything," Allison said jokingly.

"Everything is complete with this," Jan said, staring at the ornament.

The moment was interrupted when the doorbell rang.

"That must be the pizza," Allison said.

* * *

Jan and Allison ate pizza, drank wine, decorated the tree, and listened to holiday music.

"Hey, there's one more ornament left in the box," Jan said as she reached for it.

"No!" Allison blurted, but it was too late. Jan had the ornament in her hand. It was a St. Thomas ornament. "I didn't want you to see that. I didn't plan to put it on the tree. It was almost seven years ago, and life has moved on for both of us."

Jan just stared at the ornament. Allison took it out of her hand and threw it in the trash, and it shattered.

"You didn't have to do that," Jan said.

"Yes, I did," Allison said sternly.

Jan gave Allison a weak smile and said, "We need to replace it with this one."

Together, they put the "Best Friends" ornament on the tree.

"Keep it for me until I get back," Jan said softly.

"I will. And Jan, this trip will be a good thing for you," Allison said.

"I know. That's what you've told me . . . many times," Jan said. "But I wish you were coming with me. What are you going to do? Be alone during Christmas?"

"Actually, no," Allison replied. "Lambert's sister invited me to spend the holidays with her and her family, but I decided to do something that I've never done. I'm going to attend a Christmas Eve church service, and on Christmas Day I'm volunteering and serving meals down at the Church Community Center. I've already signed up for it."

"Really?" Jan asked.

"Yes. I think that it'll be good for me. I'll be doing something for others," Allison said as she poured the remaining wine into their glasses.

"No more for me. I really should be going," Jan said and headed to the door. "Lisa's going to be picking me up early, and by mid-afternoon, I'll be basking in the Belize sunshine."

"You could show a little more enthusiasm," Allison said teasingly. "And when you get there, text me, and keep me posted on all your fun."

"Okay. I'm excited!" Jan lied. "And I'll text you and let you know all about it. And you text me pictures of the foot of snow."

As Jan walked out the door, Allison yelled out to her, "I will. And if you find yourself having a miserable time, just come back home and we'll go sleigh riding!"

Jan smiled and waved goodbye.

Chapter 12

Lisa arrived at Jan's home at exactly 5:00 a.m. to pick her up for the journey to Belize. They arrived at the Tri-Cities airport, checked in, and made their way through airport security. They soon found themselves arriving at the Charlotte airport for their connecting flight.

"You're too quiet Jan," Lisa said as they made their way through the terminal for the connecting flight to Belize.

"It's just that it's been a long time since I've stepped foot in this airport," Jan replied.

"We need to get you a cocktail to calm those nerves," Lisa said with a smile. "But we'll have to wait until we get on the plane. We have to move quickly to make the connection."

They ran and finally arrived at their connecting gate.

"We made it," Lisa said with a sigh. "They're just starting the boarding, and we're priority passengers."

She charged through the line of passengers waiting to board. "Excuse me. Pardon me. Excuse us. Pardon us. Thank you."

Jan tagged along, walking quickly beside her.

Lisa held her phone up so the flight attendant could read it. The attendant said, "Yes. Thank you. You both may board."

Lisa rushed down the ramp to the plane's door. Jan followed quickly behind her. They got on the plane, and Lisa held her phone up to another flight attendant.

"Go to your left," the flight attendant instructed.

Jan followed Lisa. "*Wow*. First class?" she asked.

"Actually, business class. Do you want the window seat or the aisle seat?" Lisa asked, but before Jan could answer, "You can have the window seat. You'll love seeing the view as we land in Belize."

"Sounds good to me," Jan said.

They quickly stored their carry-ons, got comfortable, and ordered cocktails.

"This is what I call First Class," Jan said, looking over at Lisa.

"Girl, you ain't seen anything yet!" Lisa said, laughing.

"Where are the other people who signed up for this trip?" Jan asked.

"There's a couple on this flight, but most of them are on a later flight, flying coach," Lisa replied with a wink. "I wanted to get to the island early so I can greet everyone and direct them to their rooms. Remember, you get the same perks I do. You're with me. And our vacation is just getting started."

The captain interrupted Lisa with a welcoming greeting to the passengers and flight information and a soothing comment. "Just sit back and relax and we'll be arriving in Belize soon!"

Chapter 13

After arriving at the Belize airport, Jan felt more excited than she had in a long time. As she and Lisa exited the plane, Lisa said, "Follow me. We'll pick up our luggage, and we'll be on our way."

They made their way to the baggage terminal and waited for their bags to hit the carousel. There were so many bags and travelers, but Jan saw her suitcase first. "It made it," she announced to Lisa as she picked it up.

"Well, mine has to be close," Lisa said. "There it is!" She picked up her bag. "Follow me. We have private transportation waiting."

When they walked out the airport doors and into the taxi area, there was a gentleman who waved at Lisa and reached for the luggage. "Ladies, right this way. And Lisa, you're looking fine! Great seeing you again!"

"Jan, meet Henry. He's our private chauffeur, and we'll be getting in this car here . . . the black limousine. Henry, you're the best!" Lisa said.

"Limousine?" Jan asked as Henry opened the car doors for them.

"Yes. It'll be a short ride to the end of the airport," Lisa said, smiling.

"What do you mean? Won't we be flying over to the private island?" Jan asked curiously.

"Oh yes. Everyone will be flying to the island, but you and I will be taking the resort's helicopter," Lisa said with a big grin. "Told you, Jan. You're with me, and you get the same perks as I do."

"Helicopter?" Jan exclaimed. "I've never ridden in a helicopter!"

"You'll be fine. Let your vacation begin!" Lisa replied joyfully.

The ride to the other end of the airport was a short fifteen minutes with Henry driving in and out of the traffic. Once there, Henry parked the car and opened the doors for the ladies. He instructed them to wait until he got the luggage from the trunk, and then he handed the bags to the two men waiting outside the helicopter.

"Ladies, let me have your personal items, and I'll put them on the helicopter for you," Henry said, and Lisa handed her and Jan's personal bags to him.

"I'm nervous," Jan said, uncertainty in her voice.

"Just remember to follow me," Lisa instructed. "And it'll only be about fifteen to twenty minutes. I promise it'll be okay."

Henry motioned for them to board the helicopter. "Have a safe and short flight," he said with a smile, waving goodbye.

Lisa and Jan got in and sat down, and the helicopter lifted from the ground with a slight jerk.

"Sit back and close your eyes," Lisa said. "If you feel like you're going to be sick, that will help."

"I just can't believe this," Jan said. "I'm okay. Just excited!"

The clear blue skies welcomed the helicopter, and in less than twenty minutes, they landed on a large helicopter pad. Once the propellers had stopped, the door opened, and the ladies stepped out.

"What do you think?" Lisa asked.

"Lisa! This is spectacular!" Jan answered.

"You ain't seen nothing yet! Over to the right is the small hotel for guests. About seventy-five rooms. Down at the marina are forty-one two-bedroom huts for guests. And what you see on the hilltop there . . . that is the main house and hotel. That's where you and I will be staying. The owners live on the very top floor. There are three floors with conference rooms, and there's a dining room on the bottom floor. All with an ocean-front view! Except for its bright Caribbean colors, doesn't it remind you of the Biltmore Estate in Asheville?" Lisa said.

"It's a grand hacienda!" Jan said, breathless. "This is magnificent!"

A golf cart pulled up to the ladies, and the driver said, "Lisa, it's good to see you again! And who is your guest?"

"Hi, José. This is my friend Jan. She's with me," Lisa said, winking.

"Would you like to check in, or do you want a tour for your friend?" José asked.

"Let's check in. I don't think I want to overwhelm her too much on her first day," Lisa said, smiling.

The ladies were driven to the front entrance of the hotel. Immediately, bell hops gathered their luggage, and opened the front doors for them to enter the lobby. Lisa walked up to the reservation counter and handed the reservationist her business card.

"Yes, Lisa. It's so great to see you! Your rooms are ready. Here are your access cards. You know where your room is, and your guest's room is beside yours," the reservationist said.

Lisa motioned for Jan to follow her. They got on the elevator, and Lisa used her access card and pressed the button for the third floor.

"I thought the third floor was only for the owners," Jan said.

"Yes. The east wing is their residence but located in the center are their business offices. And the west wing is for special guests. We're special guests," Lisa said confidently. "And you're with me. We'll get checked in, freshen up, and get something to eat. I'm hungry, and I bet you are, too."

When they got off the elevator on the third floor, they were immediately facing a receptionist.

"Hi, Lisa. Welcome back! Who is your guest?" the receptionist asked.

"This is my friend Jan Foster," Lisa replied.

"It's a pleasure meeting you, Jan," the receptionist said, then tapped a button on her desk that opened the large double doors at the end of the hall. "Your rooms are ready for you, and you'll be able to access them with your cards now."

Jan followed Lisa down the hallway.

"Here we are," Lisa said. She used the access card and opened the door to Jan's room.

Jan gasped as she walked into her room. "Look at this view! An endless ocean view! And this room! It's a condo! I love this! Never in my wildest dreams did I imagine this place to be like this!" Jan said.

"I know. It's incredible," Lisa agreed. "Okay. It's about three, so what about . . . an hour? Is that enough time to change and freshen up? We'll go downstairs and get a bite."

"Yes. That's perfect!" Jan replied.

Lisa walked out and closed the door behind her, and Jan immediately texted Allison a picture of her room.

Jan texted: Look at my view! Look at my room! Wish you were here! 80°

Allison quickly replied back: I'm jealous! It's starting to snow. 30°

Jan texted: Miss you and love ya.

Allison replied: Miss you and love ya, too! Have fun!

Chapter 14

The next day was Christmas Eve, and the resort was ready for a festival. There were fun family events scheduled, and beautiful decorations could be found everywhere you looked. Local families arrived on the island around 4:00 p.m., anticipating Santa Claus's arrival. He would be handing out toys and gifts to the children at 6:00 p.m. Heavy hors d'oeuvres and drinks were being provided to all of the guests.

Lisa had told Jan that she would be on her own until mid-afternoon on Christmas Eve, as she would be busy helping her guests check in. So, around 2:00 p.m., Jan hopped in the shower and got dressed so she could attend the evening's celebration.

Jan heard her phone beep.

Lisa texted her: Will come to your room at 3:30. Meet hotel owners.

Jan texted back: Meet hotel owners? Don't understand.

As soon as the message was sent, Jan's phone rang. It was Lisa.

"Hey," Jan answered.

"Jan, I want you to meet the hotel owners. I was thinking that if you could meet them, they might be interested in buying a ton of books to give to the local children. What do you think? It's just a thought," Lisa asked excitedly.

"Oh wow! What a fantastic idea!" Jan replied.

"Well, with this evening's event, it'll be a brief introduction, but it'll be good timing. I'll meet you at your room at three-thirty. Are you dressed?" Lisa asked.

"Yes. Ready!" Jan answered.

"Great! See you shortly," Lisa said.

Jan walked out on the terrace and was hypnotized by the sight of the waves in the ocean. *This is so beautiful. Jackson would have loved this*, she thought.

Within thirty minutes, Lisa showed up at her door.

* * *

"Follow me," Lisa instructed Jan.

"You've been saying that a lot lately," Jan giggled.

Lisa and Jan walked past the west wing's empty receptionist area and went over to the double doors at the end of the hall.

"I'm sort of nervous about this, Lisa. What are they like?" Jan asked Lisa as they made their way down the hallway.

"Well, they're friendly, and don't be nervous. I'll make introductions, and we'll make a quick exit since they are needed downstairs for the celebration," Lisa said.

Lisa used her access card, and the double doors opened. They walked into a lobby area with another receptionist.

"Hi, Lisa. Are Mr. Harrington and Mr. Montgomery expecting you?" the receptionist asked.

"Yes. Mr. Harrington is," Lisa answered professionally.

The receptionist pressed a button on her desk, and a door across the room opened. Lisa and Jan walked through the door and found themselves in a large living room with two sofas, chairs and a combination of a bar and kitchen area, all with side doors opened that allowed the breeze from the ocean danced through the room. The direct view of the ocean was breathtaking.

"Lisa, what a pleasure it is to see you again! And who is your friend?" Mr. Harrington asked.

"Yes, Mr. Harrington, it's good to see you, too! I know that this evening is a very busy time for you, so I don't want to take much of your time. But I wanted you to meet my friend Jan Foster," Lisa said.

"Of course. My pleasure," Mr. Harrington said in a soft voice, briefly shaking Jan's hand. "Are you enjoying your stay here, Ms. Foster?"

"Oh yes," Jan answered. She was simply captivated by Mr. Harrington's eyes, his striking good looks, and his accent.

"Wonderful!" Mr. Harrington answered.

"Mr. Harrington, Jan works for a book publisher, and I thought, Mr. Harrington, that you might be interested in speaking with her about ordering children's books for the children of Belize. You and your business associate do so much for the schools on the island, so I thought that you might want to discuss this opportunity with her," Lisa said, shyly.

"What a wonderful idea," Mr. Harrington answered. "I think that would be splendid. Since now is not a good time to talk, why don't you join me for dinner the day after Christmas, Ms. Foster? We can discuss this opportunity. Maybe my business associate can join us."

"I would love the opportunity," Jan said, trying not to be overly excited.

"I have a better idea. Meet me at the marina at six the day after tomorrow, and I'll take you out for a private showing of the island. You can see the resort from the ocean's point of view. We'll have dinner and a discussion. Just look for the boat with the name '*Gone in the Wind*,'" Mr. Harrington said.

Jan was smitten. "Yes. Sounds great!"

"Well, please excuse me now, ladies. I must get downstairs before my guests start to think that Santa Claus is a no-show," Mr. Harrington said with a wink.

"Thank you, Mr. Harrington," Lisa said.

"Yes, thank you! And I look forward to dinner and discussion," Jan said, almost blushing.

Jan and Lisa walked out the door, through the lobby, and through the double doors, which shut behind them.

"Lisa, did you just set me up with this guy?" Jan asked, giggling.

"Well, maybe. But you've got to admit he's easy on the eyes," Lisa said with a laugh.

"There's something about his eyes," Jan said. "And he's such a gentleman. Do you think it's okay to do this? I thought he was married."

"Where did you get that idea?" Lisa asked. "I never told you he was married. And yes, it's okay. What's wrong with mixing a little business with a little pleasure?"

"But it's a date," Jan answered apprehensively. "I haven't been on a real date since—"

Lisa interrupted her, asking, "Don't you think that it's about time?"

Chapter 15

Allison – Christmas Day

Allison woke up around 9:00 a.m. on Christmas Day. She made her way to the kitchen and fixed a cup of coffee. She'd attended the Christmas Eve church service at midnight the night before, and she'd really felt at peace after the service. Preacher Hess, who'd conducted Lambert's memorial service, held the Christmas Eve service. She was glad that she'd attended, but she hadn't gotten home until about 2:00 a.m.

She sipped her coffee and looked outside. *Oh my! I guess the weatherman was right this time!* she thought. The snow was really coming down. She turned on the television and flipped over to the local news.

The weather reporter announced, "Today's weather doesn't look too good for traveling. It's best to stay indoors today if possible. The snowstorm arrived early this morning, and we are anticipating a foot or more of snow in the region. Latest reports show that areas in the higher elevations already have five inches. This storm doesn't look like it will clear out until tomorrow afternoon. The roads are not clear, and snowplows and salt trucks will be working around the clock to clear the roads. But the snow is really coming down and–"

Allison turned off the television. "I get the point," she said out loud. "So now what?"

She decided she would put on Christmas music, take a shower, and get dressed. She had signed up for community service today, but with the weather, she wasn't sure about getting out on the roads.

She was refilling her coffee cup when she heard the doorbell. *Who could that be?* she thought. She rushed to the door and opened it. It was Preacher Hess.

"Good morning, and Merry Christmas," Preacher Hess said.

A little startled, Allison answered, "Yes. Merry Christmas."

"I hope that I'm not disturbing you. I'll be working at the Church Community Center, and I noticed you had signed up to volunteer today. I was wondering if I could give you a ride there," Preacher Hess said.

"Well…yes, but I'm not dressed yet," Allison said apologetically.

"No problem. I will be back in an hour if that's good with you," Preacher Hess said.

"Okay. That's good. But do you really think there will people to serve in this weather?" Allison asked.

"There will be people there *because* of this weather. Some of the people are homeless, and with this weather the center will probably serve as a shelter for most of them. I'll be back to get you in about an hour," Preacher Hess said.

* * *

The center stayed steady with families, men, women, and children of all ages coming through for a Christmas dinner. Though the roads were covered with snow and dangerous to travel, people still came. It was clear that the center was serving a need, and Allison was happy that she had volunteered.

Allison was clearing away the empty serving trays when Preacher Hess approached her. "It's seven-thirty, and most of the volunteers are ready to head home. But if you get home and don't have electricity, I might be bringing you back here," he said with a smile.

"Well, I do have a generator, so hopefully it'll work. I'm ready, but I'm gonna grab a plate of food to take with me."

"Yes, by all means," Preacher Hess replied.

* * *

The roads were completely covered in snow, so Preacher Hess said a prayer before he drove out of the parking lot. *We need all the prayers we can get*, Allison thought. Preacher Hess drove slowly, but eventually arrived at her house.

"Here you are, Miss Allison. Got you home safe and sound," the preacher said proudly. "Thank you for helping us today."

"Thank you. I hope you and the others get home safely, too," Allison said as she hopped out of the large four-wheel-drive truck.

Allison headed to her front door and went inside. She was glad to be home. It had been sad to see so many people hurting during Christmas. She said a silent prayer of thanks.

She looked at her Christmas tree and thought of the events of the previous year, including the passing of Lambert. Suddenly, she felt alone. She walked into the kitchen, opened a bottle of wine, and poured herself a glass, and put the plate of food in the refrigerator. *Later*, she thought. She went back to the living room and stared at the Christmas tree. *Lambert would've enjoyed doing this today*, she thought. *He would've loved talking to the people.*

With her glass of wine in hand, Allison walked into her study, which served as a home office, too. She sat down at the desk she'd taken from Lambert's condo. She looked at it and thought of all the times he must have sat at it. She glanced over at his safe and thought, *Now is a good time to try to open it. Why not?* She got up, walked over, and turned the knob a few times. *What numbers would he have used? His birthday?* she thought. She tried it. *Nope, that didn't work. What about my birthday?* She tried those numbers. *Nope, that didn't work.*

She tried several different combinations but had no success. She was about to give up when she heard what sounded like Lambert's voice. *The most important date of my life is when I met you.*

Allison thought, *Our anniversary!* She hesitated but then turned the knob slowly to the right, then left, then right, and then back to zero. *Click!* The safe opened. Chills ran down her spine, and she jumped back as if she'd been shocked. *Holy crap!* she thought. *I just opened Lambert's safe!*

Allison picked up her glass of wine and headed to the kitchen for a refill. "Do I really want to know what's in there," she asked herself out loud. She took a couple sips of wine, and answered, "Yes, I do."

She walked back into the study and looked in the safe. Inside was a large envelope. She pulled it out and was surprised to see her name written on the outside of the envelope. She carried it over to the desk and sat down, then carefully started to open it.

Boom! The electricity went out. "What the …?" she said out loud. Within a minute, she heard the noise from the generator.

Well, that's good to know, she thought. *The one thing that Brandon left with me: a working generator.*

Allison grabbed her wine and the envelope and walked to the living room. She heard a beep from her phone. The text message alert read: WEATHER ADVISORY. POWER OUTAGES THROUGHOUT THE REGION FOR UNDETERMINED TIME. SEEK SHELTER.

"Seek shelter. Really?" Allison said loudly.

She sat in front of the fireplace, looking at the envelope. She was slowly starting to pull the contents out when she heard the doorbell. "Now what?" she asked as she stood up and made her way to the door. When she opened it, Preacher Hess was there.

"Hi, Allison. I'm headed back to the center because of the power outages. They have a generator, and many of the volunteers are now in need of heat themselves. I thought you might want to join us," Preacher Hess said.

"Well, I think I'll be okay, with my fireplace. And the generator seems to be working," Allison replied. "I can just call you if things get bad."

"Not exactly. Have you tried to make a call on your cell phone? Towers must be down. Texting is okay, but calls are not going through," Preacher Hess stated.

"Oh my! I didn't know, but I think I'll stay here," she said.

"Okay, if you're sure. But here's my cell number. Text me if you need anything. Okay?" Preacher Hess said and handed her a piece of paper with his cell phone number on it.

"Thank you," she said.

Allison closed the door, wondering if she had made the right decision. *I have my wine, and with my fireplace I won't get cold, even if the generator cuts out*, she thought.

She made her way to the living room and turned on the television, and it worked. She found a local station and put it on mute, hoping it would help with her loneliness. She sat down on the sofa and grabbed the envelope again, finally pulling out the contents. It was a letter.

My Sweet Allison,

If you are reading this, then I have said goodbye to my living on this earth and hello to living my eternity. There is or was so much that I wanted to tell you, Allison, but didn't know how, and I'm sorry you are finding it out this way. It seemed every time I had the nerve to tell you, something stopped me. I just hope and pray that you understand what I'm about to share with you.

Do you remember the first time we met? I stopped by to see Brandon, and when I walked into the office, you turned around from your desk and said hello. I fell in love with you at that moment. Your eyes grabbed me and touched my very soul. Your smile showered me with such kindness that my heart melted. If you recall, I stumbled and couldn't speak for a few seconds. No one had ever shaken my world with just a look like you did. For me, it was love at first sight. But Brandon was a friend and a business associate, and he never knew how I felt about the woman he called ' his beautiful lady.'

Did you ever wonder why I stopped by each week? It was usually about business, but sometimes it was just to see you. I realized as time went on, Brandon never really told you the truth about our business connection. You were not aware. The excuse for me to stop by was that I was giving him leads or just passing by on my way somewhere else. But Brandon and I did have a business connection. You see, I was a mule for him and Jackson. If you don't know what that means . . . well, it means that I delivered cash to people for them. Dirty money. Laundering. It was more for Jackson, but Brandon took care of getting the money prepared and giving me instructions for delivery. I never delivered any drugs, always just cash. Yes, they laundered money for the cartel. I got involved because they knew I traveled a lot with my investigate work. Brandon contacted me and offered me good pay, so I accepted. I kept a low profile, and Brandon insisted that I never get my hands dirty. I did play straight and never asked questions. I just did what I was asked to do. All those scuba diving trips that Jackson and Brandon took were not always about scuba diving.

I felt that both of them were getting over their heads and in too deep. I was trying to slowly remove myself from the situation when Brandon called me and asked that I make one last run. He said that it would be the last delivery he would have for me. I was relieved and never asked why. I just thought he sensed I wanted to quit. A week before your St. Thomas trip, Brandon and I met. He handed me a package and told me that once you all were in St. Thomas, he wanted me to put this package in his safe at the office. I know that you found it. It had a note and money in it. I never knew exactly what was written on the note, but I knew it was there. That was why you never saw it in there before you left. That was my last run for him.

Allison, I am so sorry. I wanted you to know what I know, but I was afraid you would never forgive me. I just couldn't risk losing you, the love of my life. You are (were) my everything!

So, what did happen to Brandon and Jackson? After they disappeared, I was contacted by a friend of a friend. I think the friend of a friend was really close to the cartel. He wanted me to investigate their disappearances. I went to Charlotte a few times but really didn't want to get involved, so I simply pretended to come up empty handed, and after a few visits this friend never asked me to investigate again. I figured the brothers could have stolen money from the cartel, and I certainly didn't want to get involved if they had.

But my thoughts and suspicions told me that they are still alive.

You see, Jackson wanted me to find a plastic surgeon in Argentina a year before your St. Thomas trip. He paid me to fly down there and investigate this doctor. His name was Tomas. The doctor was well known and had a reputation for giving people a new start in life. I think that's what happened. I think Brandon and Jackson got a new start in life.

And there is another reason I think Brandon and Jackson are alive. The airport camera shows them going into a bathroom but never coming out. They did come out, though. They were wearing disguises and had fade IDs. They had their disguises and different travel bags in their luggage. They dumped their luggage in the trash and walked out of the bathroom as different men carrying different travel bags. Strange that no one investigating noticed that these two men were never seen going in, only going out. That was when I knew—they're alive.

I cannot begin to know how you are feeling when you read this, but know that I loved you so much that I couldn't risk you finding Brandon and leaving me. I was selfish. I wanted you for myself. I know that you always carried a special place in your heart for Brandon, but it never stopped me from loving you. I never wanted what we shared to end. I guess this is my end, so I want you to live your life remembering all our fun times. Do not hate me. Please do not let your love for me turn into hatred. I have left this world, or you wouldn't be reading this, and I know that I died loving you with my heart and soul. Please forgive me.

Loving you in eternity,
Lambert

Allison threw the letter on the floor, collapsed on the sofa, and cried, eventually crying herself to sleep.

Chapter 16

Allison – December 26

The next day, Allison was awakened by the doorbell. *Who is that?* she thought. She made her way to the door and opened it, and there stood Preacher Hess.

"I . . . are you . . . it seems . . . Ms. Allison . . . I'm sorry. Are you okay?" Preacher Hess stammered.

"Yes. I fell asleep on the sofa last night, and you just woke me up. I'm sorry. I guess I look like a mess," Allison said, trying to be cheerful and hoping he didn't smell the alcohol on her breath.

"I'm sorry. It's ten-thirty, and I thought that you would be up by now. I just stopped by to see if you would help us at the center again today. But if it's not good timing for you, I do understand. I'm so sorry to have disturbed you," Preacher Hess said apologetically.

"No. If you'll give me an hour to shower and dress, I'd be happy to help again," Allison said, combing her hair with her fingers.

"If it's okay, I will come back in an hour. Okay?" Preacher Hess asked.

"Yes. I'll be ready," Allison answered. She smiled and closed the door.

Allison walked into the bathroom and looked at herself in the mirror. *Holy crap! I look like a witch on Halloween*, she thought. *My makeup's everywhere. There's black mascara streaked down my cheeks. I'm surprised I didn't give Preacher Hess a heart attack with my appearance,* Allison thought and giggled as she undressed and stepped in the shower.

When she was out of the shower and dressed, Allison wondered if she should call Jan and tell her about the letter. *Jan needs to know what Jackson and Brandon did to us,* she thought. *It's clear they walked away from both of us.*

* * *

The doorbell rang, and Allison grabbed her handbag and picked the letter up off the floor, stuffing it in her purse. "Coming," she yelled. And out the door she went.

After a short drive, she and Preacher Hess arrived at the center. There, she stayed so busy serving food, washing bed linens, and keeping people comfortable that she had little time to think about Lambert's letter. It had been a very busy day.

"Allison, it's almost seven. Are you ready to head home?" Preacher Hess asked.

"Do you mind if I use your office phone? Cell phones still aren't working well, and I need to make a call," Allison said.

"Sure. The phone's on the desk. Take your time," Preacher Hess said.

Allison walked into the center's office and closed the door. She picked up the phone and thought, *Should I call Jan?* After a moment of hesitation, she dialed Jan's cell number.

There were a couple of rings, and then Jan answered, "Hey! Merry Christmas, Happy New Year, and Happy Holidays!" She giggled.

"Well, just how much of the Christmas cheer have you had to drink?" Allison asked with a laugh.

"I must admit, the cocktails here are sooo tasty! I wasn't sure who was calling me, though," Jan admitted. "Where are you calling from? The caller ID shows unknown."

"Oh, I'm calling from the Church Community Center. I'm using the landline here. Cell phone service is spotty, but I thought I would call instead of texting. Are you doing okay?" Allison said.

"Guess what!" Jan said enthusiastically.

"What? This must be good!" Allison said.

"I have a date!" Jan squealed.

"A date? A real date? With a man?" Allison asked in surprise.

Jan laughed. "Yes! He is one of the owners of the resort, and Lisa introduced us!"

"I am thrilled to hear this," Allison confirmed. "When is this date with Mr. Wonderful?"

"Tomorrow evening. He has invited me to dinner, and he might be interested in buying books for the children here."

"So, is it a business dinner or a real date?" Allison asked with skepticism.

"Well . . . both, really. He is taking me out on his yacht to tour the island, and we'll have dinner on his yacht," Jan answered. "I guess I shouldn't be so excited. But he's so good-looking. He has wonderful manners and a heart-melting accent. I'm so glad that I came on this trip. I wish you were here."

Allison listened to Jan's excitement and knew that she couldn't tell her about Lambert's letter. *She deserves happiness*, Allison thought.

"Girl, you don't need me there! Sounds like you got things going on. I'm so happy for you! You'll have to give me all the juicy details," Allison said.

"Oh, I will! And are you okay?" Jan said. "You sound a little funny."

"I'm fine. Just tired. Been helping here at the center. It's been good for me to get out. And the snow here set a record. The storm has knocked out the power and cell towers, and the roads are a mess. If it weren't for Preacher Hess, I wouldn't have been able to get out. I was just thinking about you, and I had the opportunity to call to wish you Merry Christmas. Glad I did!" Allison said.

"Me, too! It's really good to talk to you," Jan said.

"Well, I better go. I'm on their phone," Allison said. "Now, you text me and tell me all juicy details about the date! And hopefully, cell phone calls will work by then. Talk care! Love you!"

"You know it! Love you, too! Merry Christmas! I'll call ya," Jan said. "Bye!"

"Bye!" Allison answered, then hung up the receiver. *Gee, she sounded so happy. Well, it's way past due*, she thought.

Allison walked out of the office and motioned to Preacher Hess that she was ready to go home. They left the center, got in his truck, and headed to her house. The roads were still messy and slippery, but Preacher Hess was a cautious driver and got Allison home safely.

"I don't know how to thank you for all you've done at the center over the last few days. I really do appreciate your help," Preacher Hess said as he stopped in Allison's driveway.

"No problem. And that phone call was long distance. I put ten dollars on the office desk for you," Allison said, smiling. "Thank you for allowing me to use the phone."

"Ten dollars? *Wow*! I'm sure it won't be that much," Preacher Hess replied. "But thank you!"

"Let me know if you need me to help anymore," Allison said as she got out of the truck. "Have a good evening."

As soon as Allison walked inside, the loneliness hit her. *I'm going to shower and go to bed. I'm exhausted, and I can feel sorry for myself tomorrow*, she thought. *I'm done with men!*

* * *

The next morning, Allison slept late. The emotional rollercoaster had taken its toll on her. When she woke, she looked at the clock and saw it was 11:30 a.m. *Guess I should get up*, she thought. *Or maybe I'll wait until Preacher Hess knocks at the door.* She snickered, then decided to go back to sleep.

It was mid-afternoon when Allison got out of bed. She showered and turned on the television. The weather reports were saying that the road conditions were improving and that power services were being restored. She had not eaten anything all day and decided to eat the leftovers from yesterday. She went to the kitchen, opened a bottle of wine, and put the leftovers in the microwave. She poured herself a glass of wine, went back to the living room, took Lambert's letter out of her purse. She sat down on the sofa and read the letter again. She didn't cry.

Lambert loved me, she thought. *How could Brandon just leave me?*

Allison glanced at the Christmas tree and Jan's ornament and thought, *Jan must be getting ready for her date with Mr. Wonderful!*

Her thoughts were interrupted by the ding of the microwave. She folded the letter and put it back in her purse.

"I think I'll watch a good movie tonight, like *Gone with the Wind*," she said out loud.

Chapter 17

Jan in Belize

The weather was beautiful and just perfect for an early sailing and maybe turning into a midnight sailing excursion. Jan was dressed and ready to head out the door. She was nervous but excited at the same time. She picked up her phone and texted Lisa.

Jan: Nervous. Excited. Meeting Mr. Harrington. On my way!

Lisa immediately texted her back: No need to be nervous. Good guy. His name is Winston. Enjoy! Have fun!

Jan took a quick last look in the mirror. Her skin glowed with the help of a bronzer and her new found tan. She adjusted her off the shoulder top and her white pants with her navy belt and then said out loud, "Ships ahoy!"

Jan left the hotel, walked to the marina, and looked for the yacht with the name "Gone in the Wind." It couldn't be missed. It was stunning.

"You're right on time," Winston yelled to her, smiling.

When she walked over, he took her hand and helped her as she stepped onto the yacht.

"This is quite a yacht, Mr. Harrington," Jan said with excitement.

"Please call me Winston," he replied.

"Okay, Winston. This is bigger than most houses! Tell me about the yacht's name. 'Gone in the Wind'? Dare I ask what that means?" Jan asked.

"Actually, the yacht is small in comparison to most. But this is my private vessel; it's not for all my guests. And the name? Well, it's a fun name. Gone for the day. Gone for the evening. Gone in the wind. And for this evening, we're gone in the wind sailing! We'll have a full galley staff onboard, and they're here to serve us. And I hope you like tonight's menu," Winston said proudly, holding her hand. "Welcome aboard."

The waitstaff greeted Jan and Winston with glasses of champagne.

"This way," Winston instructed Jan.

Jan followed him down the stairs to the cabin, which was a full and luxurious living room.

"Would you like a tour as we prepare to sail?" Winston asked.

"Oh yes!" Jan answered.

Winston was the perfect tour guide. He explained the yacht as if he were having it rebuilt. But Jan was so taken by his style, appearance, and mannerisms that it was hard for her to concentrate on the conversation, especially as she listened to his accent.

"I believe we are getting ready to sail. Let's go up to the top and watch the sun set," Winston suggested. "And I believe we are ready for another drink."

They made their way to the terrace and sat at a table with a white linen tablecloth and two place settings.

"Sir, another glass of champagne?" the steward asked.

"Let's open a bottle of wine. I hope you like red," Winston said.

"Perfect," Jan replied.

The wine was served, and they both watched the sun set as the yacht slowly moved away from the marina and out into the ocean. They made small talk, but then Winston changed the subject to business.

"Tell me more about your work, Jan," Winston said.

"I work for a small book publishing company. I love my work, and I hope that you'll be interested in buying some of our children's books, especially considering all you do here for the children," Jan replied. "The books could be donated to the local children."

The conversation was interrupted when a server came out.

"Oh, here are our appetizers," Winston said. "Caviar, cooked sushi, house-made crackers, cheese, and more. I hope this is acceptable."

"More than acceptable," Jan said shyly.

As the yacht traveled across the water, the full moon rose slowly in the sky, shining brightly on the waves. The two of them enjoyed the appetizers and a large meal. More wine and more conversation made the evening perfect.

The steward cleared the table when Winston instructed, "We'll have dessert in the cabin, so do not serve it until we are there."

Winston motioned for the steward to leave, then grabbed the wine bottle and topped off her glass. She noticed a scar on his hand.

"That's a nasty scar you have there," Jan said.

Winston hesitated. He poured the remaining wine into her glass and his glass and set down the empty bottle. He took her hand in his and opened his hand to show her his palm. She stared. She froze. She couldn't breathe. She had flashbacks of seeing Jackson's hand when it had been severely cut at his retirement party. She gasped and looked into Winston's eyes.

He leaned over her shoulder and whispered in her ear, "I still love you."

"Jackson?" Jan choked in a whisper.

"Don't be afraid, Jan. But yes. I'm Jackson, but now I'm Winston," Jackson (Winston) said quietly.

Jan stood up and backed away from the table, completely in shock. "You? All this time. How could you? I don't understand!" she yelled. "I thought you were dead!" She was going crazy. She stomped back and forth, yelling, and screaming.

"Please calm down. I can explain," Jackson (Winston) said.

He was interrupted by Jan's words. "I searched and searched for you! I loved you so much! How could you just disappear? How? I put my life on hold for you!" Jan screamed.

"Please, Jan. Calm down! Don't get so close to the edge!" Jackson (Winston) warned.

Jan didn't listen. She hastily turned and stomped back and forth like a madwoman. Suddenly, she stumbled when the yacht went over a wave that was larger than life, and she went flying over the railing of the yacht.

"Jan!" Jackson (Winston) screamed at the top of his lungs.

She was gone.

The staff ran to the terrace, and Jackson (Winston) quickly instructed the captain to anchor and contact the coast guard. The yacht stopped, and one of the staff members quickly suited up and dove into the water. Even with the brightness of the moon, the darkness of the waves had swallowed her. Jan was lost at sea.

Hours passed, seeming like an eternity.

"Keep looking. She's a good swimmer," Jackson (Winston) instructed. "Jan! Swim to us. You can do this," he yelled across the water. "Please come back!"

"I think that I'm going to have to come aboard, sir," the diver yelled to Jackson (Winston). "I've been in the water for hours."

"No!" Jackson (Winston) yelled. "You've got to find her!"

Abruptly, an announcement from the coast guard came through the captain's radio. "We've located a body…a woman. Possibly the one that went overboard. Deceased. Wearing white pants."

It was confirmed. Jan was dead.

Chapter 18

By early morning on December 28, news had spread at the resort that one of the guests had drowned. Rumors circulated, and Lisa struggled to answer her guests' questions. She didn't really know exactly what had happened.

She received a text message from her brother.

Jackson (Winston): Jan's Dead. Come now.

Lisa walked past the receptionist and stormed through the double doors leading to the private residence of Jackson (Winston) and Brandon (Buckie). Both were sitting quietly at their bar, drinks in their hands. Lisa entered, and the doors closed behind her.

"I can't believe this!" she yelled hysterically.

"Pull yourself together," Jackson (Winston) said. "It was an accident."

"Accident? How did this happen? What do I do? She was my guest. She was my friend," Lisa said desperately. "The police are here, and my guests are asking questions. I think I'm going to be sick." She flopped down on the sofa.

"Lisa, she was more than just a guest or friend to me. I loved Jan. I've always loved her," Jackson (Winston) said through tears. "I never would've had you bring her here if I had thought she would get hurt, much less…die."

"What are you telling the police?" Lisa asked, trying to stay calm.

"I don't really have to say much to them. The yacht's camera tells the story. We got into a heated discussion, and she ran to the edge of the boat, tripped, and, with the surge of a wave, fell overboard. The staff heard us, and their stories support the events on camera. The video shows everything. Shows that she tripped on her flip-flop and fell overboard, hitting her head. She was not pushed. The only question they've asked is what the argument was about. I simply told the police that she was a guest but that we had met several years ago during a one-night stand. I made a suggestion that she and I rekindle our relationship and get better acquainted, and she was offended," Jackson (Winston) answered. "With as much as we do for the community financially, I could've killed her and the police would've looked the other way. But there's nothing to hide!"

"What the hell am I going to tell Allison?" Lisa asked.

"You need to reach out to her asap. Ask her to come and help you," Jackson (Winston) said coldly. "We need to make arrangements to get her body back to the States. I've made arrangements for a cremation."

"Cremation?" Lisa said softly.

"Yes. But her remains should be returned to her family. Although, as I recall, she wasn't close to any of her family. This is why you need to reach out to Allison. She can help us," Jackson (Winston) said.

Lisa looked over at Brandon (Buckie). "Well, Mr. Buckie, you're awfully quiet," she said sarcastically.

"If you reach out to Allison, be prepared to tell her everything," Brandon (Buckie) answered harshly, speaking to both of them.

"Tell her everything? I'm not telling her a damn thing. And what do you think she's going to do? Jump overboard, too?" Lisa said bitterly.

"You knew, Lisa, that we were trying to get them here," Jackson (Winston) said calmly. "You've known all along. I just hadn't planned on losing Jan once I got her here." He broke down in tears and walked out of the room.

"Great," Lisa said, turning to Brandon (Buckie). "What do I tell Allison?"

"Tell her that there's been an accident and Jan didn't make it. Tell her as much of the truth as possible. I'll take care of the rest when she gets here. Can you make arrangements to get her here asap?" he said.

"Yes. I can pull some strings and get her here by tomorrow afternoon, *if* she's willing to come. We'll have to use the private jet," Lisa answered.

"Jan was her best friend. She'll come," Brandon (Buckie) answered assuredly. "And do what you have to do to get her here."

Lisa looked at him, shook her head, and walked out of the room.

* * *

Before calling Allison, Lisa made flight arrangements for Allison to arrive the next day. Once all the arrangements were made, she dialed Allison's number but got a recording that said, "All circuits are busy. Please try your call later."

Terrific, Lisa thought. *I'll just text her and ask her to call me.*

THIS IS LISA. CALL ME AS SOON AS YOU GET THIS. ASAP! EMERGENCY!

Chapter 19

Allison – December 28

The next morning, Allison awoke late again. When she looked at the clock, it was 11:00 a.m. *Gotta get up and run to the grocery store. Almost out of wine*, she thought.

She showered, dressed, and listened to the latest weather report. The report stated that the roads were mostly clear. The sun was shining brightly as she left the house, but it was cold. She made her way to her car, got in, and headed to the grocery store. As she drove, she passed the Community Center. She saw Preacher Hess's truck parked there and decided to buy a few extra grocery items and drop them off to Center.

* * *

By 2:00 p.m., Allison had finished her shopping and was pulling into the center's parking lot. She heard her phone beep. She parked and looked at her phone.

Lisa: THIS IS LISA. CALL ME AS SOON AS YOU GET THIS. ASAP! EMERGENCY!

Allison immediately tried to call her, but the recording came on stating that all circuits were busy.

"Gee, are they ever going to get the towers fixed?" she asked out loud.

She grabbed the bags of food for the center, got out of her car, and walked inside. She saw Preacher Hess and said, "Hey, I brought some food items. Thought you might need them."

Preacher Hess walked over to her and took the bags. "Yes! Thank you! How thoughtful and generous," he said. "We actually still have some families here with no power in their homes. This will help."

"I hate to ask, but may I use your office phone again? I received a text message, and there seems to be an emergency of sorts," Allison said.

"Of course," Preacher Hess said. "You go right ahead."

Allison walked to the office and closed the door. She dialed Lisa's phone number and anxiously waited for an answer.

"Hi. This is Lisa," Lisa answered.

"Hey, Lisa. This is Allison. I'm calling from the Church Community Center. Cell phones are not working yet. I got your text message, though. What's wrong?" Allison asked.

There was silence, and then Lisa finally said, "Allison, I need you to pack your bags and get here. I've made your flight arrangements."

"Why? What's wrong?" Allison asked again.

"It's Jan. There's been an accident. She . . . she . . . " Lisa's voice quivered. "You need to get here asap."

"Jan? Is Jan okay? You're scaring me, Lisa. What's happened?" Allison asked.

Lisa audibly swallowed and replied, "Jan is not okay. She didn't survive the accident. She's gone."

There was a long pause. "Jan is dead?" Allison finally asked softly.

"Yes," Lisa answered through tears.

Thump! Allison dropped the receiver as she passed out and hit the floor.

The noise was so loud that Preacher Hess heard the noise and ran to the office door. He opened the door slightly and saw Allison lying on the floor. "Great Mother of God!" Preacher Hess yelled. Two of the volunteers heard Preacher Hess and came running into the office.

"Quick! Get the first aid kit! It's got smelling salts in it," Preacher Hess instructed the volunteers as he tried to revive Allison.

"Allison. Allison! It's Preacher Hess. Can you hear me? Wake up, Allison!" Preacher Hess commanded, patting her face.

He was able to lift her into an upright position when a volunteer handed the smelling salts to him. "Breathe, Allison. You're going to be okay. Someone get a glass of water."

"I'm okay," Allison whispered.

"Here. Drink some water," Preacher Hess said. "What happened? Did you get some bad news or something?"

Allison pointed to the phone. Preacher Hess walked over and picked up the tangling receiver and said, "Hello."

"Hello. Preacher Hess? This is Lisa Taylor. Do you remember me?" Lisa asked.

"Oh yes, Lisa. I remember you. Jackson and Brandon's sister. Well, it seems like whatever news you gave to Allison was bad. She passed out," Preacher Hess said, sounding concerned. "What's happened?"

"Is she okay?" Lisa asked, ignoring his question.

"I think so," Preacher Hess answered. "Do you want me to get her back to the phone? I'm not sure that's a good idea, though."

"Yes. It's important," Lisa answered sternly.

Preacher Hess turned to Allison and asked, "Do you want to continue this conversation with Lisa? It's up to you."

"Yes," Allison answered weakly. She slowly stood up.

Preacher Hess handed the receiver to Allison and motioned for the volunteers to exit the office with him. Allison watched and waited for the door to close.

"Lisa. What the hell happened? Jan cannot be dead!" Allison screamed into the phone.

"Allison, I need you here. I've made arrangements to get you here tomorrow. I'll explain everything to you when you get here. Please! You are—were—Jan's closest friend, and I've got guests here that I'm responsible for. I'm trying to keep everyone calm here, and I need you here," Lisa pleaded.

"Well, I guess," Allison answered, trying to remain calm. "But what happened?"

Lisa ignored her question. "Your flight leaves early in the morning. You'll travel from the Tri-Cities to Charlotte. Then from Charlotte to Key West. Once you get into Key West, I'll meet you at the baggage claim, and we'll fly on a private jet to Belize. From there, we'll take a helicopter to the resort," she explained.

"Jan is dead?" Allison asked again.

"Yes," Lisa answered coldly. "Allison, did you understand the flight instructions?"

"Are the tickets—" Allison tried to ask, but Lisa interrupted her.

"Your tickets will be waiting for you. Just show up, Allison. I need you. And this is for Jan."

"What kind of accident?" Allison asked, holding back tears.

"I'm upset, too, so let me just explain everything when you get here," Lisa said. "But . . . basically, she fell off a boat, hit her head, and didn't survive."

"I'm heartbroken. She was my best friend," Allison said through tears.

"I understand. I thought a lot of her, too," Lisa said. "You'll be here?"

"Yes. I'll pack and fly out tomorrow. I'll see you in Key West," Allison said, gathering her composure.

"Text me if there's a problem," Lisa said.

"I will," Allison answered. "I just can't believe this."

"See you tomorrow," Lisa said, hanging up without saying goodbye.

Allison slowly put down the receiver. She stared at the phone. *How can this be?* she thought. *My best friend!* She started sobbing uncontrollably.

Preacher Hess was standing near the door. He hadn't meant to eavesdrop, but he was concerned about Allison and her reaction to the obvious unwelcome news. He opened the door and walked over to Allison. Without a word, he embraced her.

Allison let her tears flow. "My best friend is dead. She's gone. My best friend! I loved her like a sister!" she cried.

Preacher Hess remained silent.

After long minutes, and after several tissues were used, he said, "Allison, you need to sit down before you pass out again." He grabbed a chair, and Allison collapsed onto it. He grabbed another chair and sat next to her.

No words were spoken. Allison just cried.

Finally, Preacher Hess said, "I remember Jan. She and Jackson were a couple, and she was with you at Lambert's funeral."

Allison stopped crying, took a deep breath, and answered, "Yes. She's gone. There was an accident on a boat, and she's gone. I have to get home so I can pack and get to Belize."

"Are you sure you can drive, much less travel?" Preacher Hess asked.

"Yes. I just can't believe this," Allison said.

"Let me drive you home, and I can pick you up in the morning and take you to the airport," Preacher Hess offered.

"No. That's not necessary. I'm okay," Allison assured him.

"Are you sure?" he asked.

"I'm okay. Thank you for your concern," Allison said sadly. She slowly walked out of the office, and he walked behind her.

"Allison, if there is anything, and I mean *anything*, that I can do, please . . . please just tell me," Preacher Hess said.

Allison made her way to the door, turned, and faced Preacher Hess, and said, "Thank you. I'll be all right. If I need anything, I'll let you know. I promise."

Chapter 20

Allison had no trouble arriving at the airport early the next morning, as she didn't sleep much the night before. She'd just went through the motions while packing, so she hoped that she'd brought everything she needed.

She arrived at the airport, checked in and, got her boarding passes, and she soon found herself in Key West, Florida.

She looked around the baggage claim area but didn't see Lisa, so she picked up her luggage and walked through the exit doors. Lisa stood next to a limousine.

"Hey, Allison, I just got here. Guess the flights were all on time," Lisa said, trying to make small talk.

They exchanged a hug, and Allison answered, "I guess so."

"Let me take your luggage, miss," the chauffeur said, then opened the car door.

"So, where are we going now?" Allison asked.

"He'll take us to a private jet, and we'll be on our way to the Belize airport," Lisa answered. "We should be on the plane in a few minutes."

"Can you tell me about Jan?" Allison asked.

"I will. I promise. Why don't we wait until we get on the plane, though? We can have a cocktail and a snack. Have you eaten?" Lisa asked.

"No, but I did have a cocktail on the plane," Allison said.

They both remained silent until they had arrived at the private jet and were seated inside it.

"This is the way to travel," Allison said, breaking the silence.

"It's nice, isn't it?" Lisa asked.

The flight attendant approached them and asked, "Would you ladies like cocktails? Lisa, do you want your usual?"

"Yes. And bring us some light bites, too. This is Allison," Lisa answered.

"Allison, would you like a cocktail or glass of wine?" the flight attendant asked.

"I would like to have a vodka and soda, please," Allison answered. She turned to Lisa and asked, "She knows your usual? How did she know that?"

"This jet belongs to the owners of the resort, and since I do so much business traveling with them, I get special perks," Lisa said matter-of-factly.

The flight attendant brought the drinks and some small sandwiches, then left them alone again.

"So, now. Tell me what happened to Jan," Allison instructed.

"Well . . . okay. Jan was on a boat. She tripped, and with the help of a large wave, she fell overboard. As she fell, she must have hit her head. The coast guard retrieved the body," Lisa said slowly.

Allison listened intently and then asked, "So, she basically drowned?"

"Yes," Lisa said. "It was truly an accident. We both lost a very good friend."

Allison didn't ask any more questions. They both remained quiet. Allison drifted off to sleep, and Lisa found herself worried about the next few hours. *How is Allison going to react to the truth of all this?* she thought.

* * *

They arrived at the Belize airport and were quickly taken to the helicopter. After they had boarded, Allison felt excited about seeing the resort and finding out more about what the resort had to offer.

When they arrived at the resort, Lisa helped Allison check in and took her to the private floor where she had an assigned room.

"This is some place! Look at this room and this view!" Allison said with excitement after they had gone inside her room. "The resort is called 'My Beautiful Lady'? You never mentioned that."

"Well, that's its informal name. It's called Fantasy Paradise," Lisa said. "I'm sure you're tired, so why don't you rest up and freshen up. I'll see you in an hour or so. We'll grab a light dinner, and then I want you to meet someone."

"Meet someone? Who?" Allison asked.

"The resort owners. They made all the arrangements for Jan, and the arrangements to get you here, and they want to meet you," Lisa said quickly. "I'll see you in an hour." She hurried out the door.

Chapter 21

An hour later, Lisa and Allison enjoyed a meal together. Allison was more relaxed after seeing the resort. Lisa tried to make light conversation.

When they finished, Lisa signed the receipt and thanked the server, and they left the restaurant. They made their way to the private floor of the hotel and walked to the end of the hall. Lisa pushed the buzzer and swiped her card, and the double doors opened. There was no receptionist, so Lisa walked past the reception desk and swiped her card again. The next door opened. Two men were sitting at the bar in the open living room, and Lisa approached them.

"Winston, Buckie, this is Allison Hurley, Jan's best friend," Lisa said coldly.

Lisa motioned to Allison to sit down on the sofa, and she followed.

"Yes. Please have a seat, ladies," Winston (Jackson) said abruptly.

Strange introduction, Allison thought as she and Lisa sat down on the sofa.

Winston (Jackson) and Brandon (Buckie) walked over and sat on the sofa across from Lisa and Allison.

"What did you tell her, Lisa?" Winston (Jackson) asked.

"The truth," Lisa answered. "It was an accident."

Winston (Jackson) looked at Allison and asked, "Do you have any questions?"

Surprised by his question, Allison answered, "Yes. I would like to know what happened. Or rather, *how* it happened."

There was a moment of silence. Winston (Jackson) looked down at his scarred hand, and thought, *How do I tell her?*

Winston (Jackson) started by saying, "Jan joined me for a dinner date on my yacht, and—"

Allison interrupted, saying, "You were the one? The one who Jan was so excited about? The date?" She turned to Lisa and asked, "You knew this? He was the dinner date that Jan was so excited about?"

"Yes," Lisa answered.

"You knew that we had a dinner date?" Winston (Jackson) asked.

"Jan texted me. She was overly excited about the date," Allison answered quietly.

"Well, she and I were having an enjoyable evening, and . . . and—" Winston (Jackson) stopped when interrupted by Lisa.

"Just tell her," Lisa blurted out.

"Tell me what?" Allison asked.

Winston (Jackson) walked over and held out his scarred hand. Allison stared at it. She gasped. She glanced over at Buckie (Brandon) and tried to speak, but she couldn't.

"Do you recognize this scar on my hand? A scar from a drunken fall at The Martha Washington Inn?"

The room was silent. Allison just stared at Buckie (Brandon).

"By the expression on your face, I think that you do," Winston (Jackson) said, emotionless.

"I can't breathe," Allison choked.

"Get her something! Water! Anything!" Lisa yelled. "Calm down! Calm down, Allison!" She jumped to her feet. She patted Allison on the back and rubbed her hands.

Winston (Jackson) walked over to the bar and filled a glass with water. He came back over and handed it to Allison. All eyes were on her as she sat there motionless.

"Allison. I wanted to tell you but didn't know how. Yes, this is Jackson and Brandon," Lisa said, trying to console Allison. "Talk to me!"

Allison took a sip of water. "You killed my best friend!" she screamed through tears. She looked over at Buckie (Brandon). "And you ... you ..."

"Yes, I'm Brandon," he said.

"How could you? I need a drink. Make it a double," Allison said.

Buckie (Brandon) jumped up, went to the bar, and fixed a double vodka. He came back over and handed it to Allison.

She gulped it down and said, "I need another."

Buckie (Brandon) made another and brought it to her.

"Go slow, Allison," Lisa instructed as she held her hand. "You had a couple of drinks earlier, too."

"You've known all along, haven't you?" Allison asked Lisa bitterly.

Lisa didn't answer.

"I'm sorry you had to find out this way," Winston (Jackson) said.

"Well, now that I know, are you going to kill me, too?" Allison asked abruptly.

"I never killed Jan. I loved Jan with all my heart!" Winston (Jackson) yelled. He broke down in uncontrollable sobs and walked out of the room.

Lisa's phone beeped, and she read a text message. "Gotta go. Two of my guests are trying to kill the tour guide. You're on your own, Buckie! Sorry, Allison. I wish that this could have been different," she said calmly before bolting out the door.

Allison was so stunned that she couldn't move. She just sat there as she heard the door close behind Lisa. She stared at Buckie (Brandon). The silence was broken when she said sarcastically, "Your plastic surgery changed your appearance, but I still recognize you."

"We did have plastic surgery," Buckie (Brandon) confirmed. "You noticed?"

Allison reached into her handbag and tossed Lambert's letter to Buckie (Brandon). The letter fell to the floor. He picked it up and read it. After reading it, he tossed it back to her. She picked it up, folded it, and put it in her purse.

"So, he told you what he thought?" Buckie (Brandon) asked bitterly. "And he loved you."

"Oh yes! He hid this in his safe, and I found it after he died! So he kept your secret! You men … You stick together when it comes to lying to your women!" Allison cried.

"I never meant to hurt you, Allison," Buckie (Brandon) tried to explain. "But you didn't waste any time getting in bed with Lambert, did you?"

"How dare you! You left me stranded at the airport and left me to figure out what to do with the business and everything! And your note made it clear that you had left me. You told me to get on with my life. Did you think I would chase after you? Like Jan did Jackson? Chasing a ghost? Hell no! You left me…and I…I…" Allison's words faded as she stood up and then collapsed back onto the sofa.

"Allison? Allison? Are you okay?" Buckie (Brandon) asked as he ran over to her. "Oh damn! She passed out." He yelled for the butler.

"Yes, sir?" the butler asked when he came into the room.

"Bring me a blanket and pillow. And another glass of water," Buckie (Brandon) instructed.

"Yes, sir," the butler replied, hurrying off.

Allison opened her eyes to Buckie (Brandon) slapping her hands and patting her face.

"You passed out, Allison," he said softly. "Just lie here and be still."

They looked over as the butler came back in carrying a blanked, a pillow, and a glass of water. He handed everything to Buckie (Brandon).

"Thank you," Buckie (Brandon) said.

"Yes, sir," the butler said before exiting the room.

"Did you put something in my drink?" Allison asked sternly, taking the glass of water from Buckie (Brandon).

"Absolutely not! But you had two strong drinks. What did you expect?" he said, putting the pillow under her head and the blanket over her.

"Let me sit up," Allison said.

She sat up and continued to drink the water. "I do not understand how you and Jackson could have done this to Jan and me!"

"His name is Winston. And we tried to bring you both back into our lives. But one couldn't be here without the other. And you…you jumped in bed with another man. A relationship! What was I supposed to do? Winston (Jackson) and I were on the run. We did everything to get off the radar, and we had to cut ties with everyone and everything. But Lisa was our link to both of you. After things calmed down, we tried many times to get you and Jan here. Lisa kept us informed on what was going on with the two of you. And Jan… Jan refused to come here. How were we supposed to get the two of you to come here?"

"Well, I pushed her to come to this Fantasy Island, and look what happened to her!" Allison yelled.

"It was an accident," Buckie (Brandon) said quietly.

"I need to go to my room," Allison said. "I don't feel well."

"We have to talk, Allison. I'll walk you to your room, but tomorrow we have to talk about things," Buckie (Brandon) said.

"What is there to talk about?" Allison asked.

Buckie (Brandon) looked Allison in the eyes and slowly said, "Us."

"I hate you! That finishes that talk. May I go to my room now?" she asked.

Buckie (Brandon) stood up and reached to take Allison's hand. She ignored the gesture, stood up, and staggered to the door. Buckie (Brandon) slipped his arm around her waist to hold her steady. Allison felt the warmth of his touch. His arm felt so strong, and she yearned to feel his arms wrapped around her entire body. She wanted to embrace him. She stopped and thought, *No. I can't do that!*

"Here, I'll have to get the door," Buckie (Brandon) said.

Buckie (Brandon) walked Allison to her room. He opened the door and asked, "Are you going to be okay?"

She turned to him and said, “Yes!” before slamming the door in his face.

Chapter 22

The next morning, Allison woke with a really bad hangover. She looked at her cell phone. It was 10:30 a.m. *It's too early*, she thought. She rolled over and went back to sleep.

By late afternoon, Lisa realized that she had not heard from Allison or Buckie all day, so she decided to text her brother.

Lisa: Have you heard from Allison?

Buckie (Brandon) : No. u?

Lisa texted: No. Been busy. Will check on her.

Buckie (Brandon): Want me 2?

Lisa texted: No. Best I do.

Buckie (Brandon): Ok. Let me know.

Lisa finished the last project she needed to get done for tomorrow's New Year's celebration, and then she texted Allison.

Lisa: Hey u okay?

Because there was no immediate reply, Lisa went to Allison's room and knocked on the door. No answer.

She waited a few seconds, then knocked again and called out, "Allison, it's Lisa. You okay?" She heard movement, and within a few seconds Allison opened the door.

"Allison, are you okay?"

"I woke up feeling pretty bad. Bad hangover, I guess," Allison answered as Lisa walked in.

"Well, I guess so considering all that alcohol you had to drink. And you look terrible. You haven't eaten today, have you?" Lisa asked.

Allison shook her head no.

"I'll order room service. You'll feel better after you eat some food and drink some water," Lisa said.

Lisa ordered room service while Allison changed from her PJs to a pair of shorts and a top. They grabbed bottles of water from the refrigerator and walked out on the terrace.

"It's beautiful, isn't it?" Lisa asked, sitting down beside Allison.

"Lisa. You knew all along that Jackson and Brandon were alive, didn't you?" Allison asked calmly. "Why didn't you tell Jan and me?"

Lisa took a deep breath and answered, "It wasn't that simple."

"Then tell me," Allison said.

"Well, when Jackson and Brandon disappeared, I was as shocked and worried as anyone. For six months, I struggled to accept that my brothers were gone. It just didn't make sense to me. Then one day, I got a card in the mail from this resort outside Belize. The card was an invitation for me to visit so I could consider bringing vacationers there through my travel agency. I called, all the arrangements were made for me, and I showed up. I had no clue. But during dinner, they told me who they were. Winston and Buckie. And that's who they are now, Allison. In a way, Jackson and Brandon did die. Anyway, time went on, and I tried to get you and Jan to come visit this place with me. But then you and Lambert became a couple, and I couldn't push Jan into considering it."

"Lambert suspected that they were still alive," Allison interjected.

"Why? Did he tell you that?" Lisa asked.

"Not exactly," Alison answered.

"Well, Lambert did reach out to me," Lisa said. "Did you know that?"

Looking surprised, Allison answered, "No. I wasn't aware that he contacted you."

"He did. He called me, and I met him for drinks. He asked me a lot of questions. Questions that, I thought, he really shouldn't be asking. And because he was an investigator, I didn't trust him. I thought that he was setting me up with the FBI," Lisa said. "I never told him anything."

"You think that Lambert did investigative work for the FBI?" Allison asked interrupting Lisa.

"Yes. He seemed to know more than he let on. He told me that I should be careful and that the FBI was following me. He told me that they were on almost every flight that Jan took, and if they weren't on the flight, there was someone following her around at the airport. Lambert warned me to be cautious during my travels and said that I should be careful where I traveled to. He also told me that you were being followed. He said, 'Don't compromise yourself.' After that warning, I completely backed off for several months and made very little contact with Winston (Jackson) and Buckie (Brandon). Honestly, I didn't trust Lambert. I'm sorry. I think that he did do some work for the FBI, at least until they realized he hadn't found anything," Lisa said.

Allison looked at Lisa and said, "I have a letter that I want you to read." She got the letter from her purse and handed it to Lisa.

After reading it, Lisa turned pale. She handed the letter back to Allison. "He knew, Allison. He knew. He was just protecting you, Allison, because he loved you."

"But I didn't know anything," Allison said defensively. "And I'm not sure that I agree with you. He didn't disclose anything to the FBI. That, I'm sure of. He was protecting all of us."

There was a knock at the door.

"Room service," Lisa said. She jumped up, went inside, opened the door, and announced, "Room service is here."

"Thanks!" Allison said, coming inside.

"And I had an extra-large Bloody Mary prepared for you. Great hangover cure," Lisa said. "So, enjoy! Do you want company later?"

"No. I think that I'll just enjoy the food, drink, and the view," Allison answered. "I want time to just think."

"Well, rest up. Tomorrow is New Year's Eve," Lisa said.

Allison gave Lisa a blank stare.

"Goodnight! See you tomorrow," Lisa said, closing the door behind her.

Chapter 23

New Year's Eve

Allison woke up around 10:00 a.m. the next day, feeling much better than she had the day before. She fixed herself a cup of coffee and walked out onto the terrace. She watched the waves and thought, *What a beautiful day! I may never come back to this place, so while I'm here, I'm going to get some sun.*

She quickly showered, dressed, and headed down to the hotel's boutique. She bought a bathing suit, a bathing suit cover, a hat, a book, a magazine, and suntan lotion, charging it all to the room. *Guess I can charge this to my room, and the owners can pay!* she thought.

Allison made her way to the pool and found the perfect lounge chair for the day. *I think I'll stay right here all day and just watch the waves*, she thought.

She ordered drinks and lunch from the pool attendant and stayed by the pool all day.

* * *

Lisa found herself answering guests' questions and leading guests' excursions from early morning to late afternoon. Between setting up the New Year's Eve celebration and getting all the food preparation done, it was a busy day for her. It was almost 5:00 p.m. before she even thought about Allison and what she might do for the day. She texted Buckie (Brandon).

Lisa: Have you heard from Allison. Been busy all day!

Buckie (Brandon) texted: Not to worry. Allison was at pool all day. Been watching her.

Lisa texted: U been spying on her?

Buckie (Brandon): yes of course

Lisa felt better knowing that Allison had found her way to the pool. After she had wrapped up her last consultation with a guest, she walked to the pool area. It was well past 5:00 p.m., and there was no one there.

"Everyone has left to get ready for the New Year's Eve party," the pool attendant said to Lisa when she walked through the pool area.

"Yes. The band starts at eight, and the celebration will begin!" Lisa said.

She left the pool area and headed to Allison's room. She knocked on the door.

Allison opened it and said, "Hi, Lisa."

Lisa hesitated but asked, "May I come in?"

"Of course. I was just getting ready to shower. I've been at the pool all day," Allison answered neutrally.

"Good! I hope you had a good day," Lisa said, trying to be upbeat. "I know that it may seem inappropriate, but it is New Year's Eve…and I want you to join me and my guests for the celebration."

"I should be so angry with you, Lisa, but I'm not. Blood is thicker than water, and they were—are—your brothers. I just wanted you to know that. But as far as this evening and celebrating goes, no, I don't think so," Allison said with no emotion.

"Well, I do hope that you understand. I think a lot of you, just as I thought a lot of Jan. I do wish you would join us. The band is starting at eight, and there's food. It's not just couples. You can be my special guest," Lisa said.

"No. I don't think so. I can hear the band from my terrace. I'm going to shower, order room service, and have a quiet New Year's Eve," Allison replied. "And I've helped myself to the booze in the room's bar."

"Yes! By all means, help yourself," Lisa said with a wink and a smile. "Just know that you're welcome to come downstairs anytime."

Allison walked over to the room's complimentary bar and fixed herself a vodka and soda. "Want one?"

"No. Gotta get back downstairs. Also, I need to let you know that we leave in the morning at eleven. The helicopter will take us to the mainland, and we'll board the private jet to Key West, then travel on to the Tri-Cities."

"So, at eleven, we leave Fantasy Paradise?" Allison asked in a sarcastic tone.

"Yes. Unless you would like to stay," Lisa answered calmly.

Allison gave her a surprised look, then looked out to the ocean. "I don't think there's anything—or anyone—here for me."

Lisa walked to the door, turned, and said, "See ya in the morning. And Happy New Year!" She closed the door before Allison had time to reply.

As Lisa left Allison's room, she texted Buckie (Brandon)

Lisa: Allison is staying in. Ordering room service. Thought u might be able to talk with her. Plan to leave in morning at 11.

Buckie (Brandon) texted back to Lisa: Thanks. I will take the room service to her. Will talk to her.

* * *

Allison finished her drink and then called room service.

"Yes, ma'am. Will be forty-five minutes."

Forty-five minutes will give me time to shower, Allison thought.

She showered and slipped on a pair of shorts and a top, then waited on the terrace for room service to arrive. It was almost an hour before she heard a knock on the door. A man said, "Room service." She stood up to go to the door, but it flew open, and Buckie (Brandon) pushed a food cart inside the room. On it was a bottle of champagne as well as two glasses.

"Room service served, madam," Buckie (Brandon) said with a smile.

"If you're part of the room service, take it back. I didn't order it," Allison said bitterly.

Buckie (Brandon) ignored her comment and pushed the cart out to the terrace. He opened the food and there were two servings of food on the cart.

"You have to eat. And so do I," Buckie (Brandon) said. "And we need to finish our talk. We can do that over dinner."

"Do I have a choice? "Allison asked, irritated.

"No. You do not," Buckie (Brandon) said. "Here, let's eat."

"A bottle of wine? A bottle of champagne? Do you think that you'll get me drunk and then kill me?" Allison asked.

Buckie (Brandon) looked at Allison and asked, "Really?"

Allison gave him a smirk and pulled a couple of chairs over to the serving cart, and Buckie (Brandon) put the food on plates, poured the wine, and motioned for her to sit.

They ate in silence until Allison said, "I'm not sure what I'm supposed to say to you."

"Just eat and drink your wine. We have plenty of time to talk," Buckie (Brandon) answered as he ate his food.

Allison glanced over at Buckie (Brandon) as they ate their dinner. *He's so handsome,* she thought. *And yes, I still care. But it's been seven years. How could he just leave me?*

When they had finished their meals, Buckie (Brandon) refilled their wine glasses and broke the silence and asked, "Do you want to know what happened?"

"What is there to know? You and Jackson—excuse me, Winston—left your girlfriends at an airport and disappeared, and we had to face the consequences of your actions," Allison stated.

"We were getting in over our heads with the cartel. The more we did, the more they wanted us to do. But we were clean. We never sold drugs. It all started on a scuba trip. We happened to meet this guy who told us we could make a lot of money just by hiding money. We were laundering money. At first, it was just a few million, but then it turned into hundreds of millions. We wanted to get out, but we didn't see a way. It was always, 'This is the last one,' but it wasn't. Winston (Jackson) thought it was a way for us to save for our retirement," Buckie (Brandon) said when he was interrupted.

"So, all of this was his idea?" Allison asked. "You could've said no."

"I guess I could have, but it seemed like an easy way to make money. We just didn't think about it being so hard to quit. It was never about leaving you and Jan," Buckie (Brandon) said apologetically.

Allison and Buckie (Brandon) could hear the music from the band as they continued to talk and talk. It was when they heard the countdown of the old year going out and welcoming the New Year begin that Buckie (Brandon) jumped up, grabbed the champagne bottle, and quickly opened it. He poured it into their glasses.

"Happy New Year" was yelled all over the resort.

Buckie (Brandon) handed a glass of champagne to Allison. "Happy New Year!" he said, tapping his glass against hers.

Allison stared at Buckie (Brandon) and repeated his words back to him. "Happy New Year!"

"Allison, I love you. I want you to stay here. Let's spend the rest of our days as husband and wife here on this island," Buckie (Brandon) said abruptly.

Allison was taken aback by his bluntness and shocked by his words.

"Please tell me you'll stay," Buckie (Brandon) pleaded.

Allison set down her glass, looked at Buckie (Brandon) and simply said, "No." She went inside, walked to the door, and opened it. "You need to leave and move on with your life, just as you told me to do almost seven years ago. We have no future," Allison said and held onto the doorknob of the opened door.

Buckie (Brandon) walked through the door, turned, and faced Allison, and said, "Love never ends."

Allison closed the door.

Chapter 24

At 10:30 a.m. the next day, there was a knock on Allison's door. She opened it.

"Guess you're ready to go?" Lisa asked hurriedly.

"Yes. All packed," Allison answered.

When they got down to the lobby, they hopped on the golf cart, and they and their luggage were quickly whisked away to the helicopter pad. Their luggage was carried to the helicopter, and then they were told to board. Allison had hoped that Buckie (Brandon) would be there to say goodbye, but he wasn't. They hopped on the helicopter, and within a few minutes they had landed at the Belize airport. They soon departed on the private jet.

On the private jet, Allison asked, "Is Jan . . . her remains . . . Is she on board?"

"Yes. The funeral home provided that service. Her remains are packaged carefully for travel, along with all the documentation," Lisa answered.

"Are you sure?" Allison asked.

"Look behind you," Lisa answered.

Allison turned and looked at the row of seats behind her. Tucked in a seat was what appeared to be a bowling ball bag in a crate.

"A bowling ball bag?" Allison gasped.

"No, it's a designer bag for an urn," Lisa answered. "Securely strapped for the ride."

Allison said, "Okay, I guess. I think that calls for a drink!"

* * *

The flight was smooth, and Allison slept until the plane touched down in Key West, Florida.

"Guess I fell asleep," she said.

"Well, me, too," Lisa said. "We'll be here for an hour or so while they refuel and prepare for the flight to the Tri-Cities, so let's go to a restaurant and get a light bite."

"So you're flying with me to the Tri-Cities?" Allison asked.

"Yes. Josh is meeting me there, and he and I will head back to Key West, then go on to the resort for some R and R," Lisa answered.

"Oh, so you're returning and not staying–"

Lisa interrupted Allison by finishing her question. "Staying for Jan's service?"

"Well, yes," Allison replied.

"I feel so guilty that Jan came to the resort. It was because of me. I don't think that I should attend her services, and besides, I said my goodbyes to her–and shared my regrets–before you got to the resort," Lisa said, starting to cry. "I feel so guilty!"

Allison looked at her, and for the first time on the trip, she felt sorry for Lisa. She had been so concerned about herself and her own guilt that she hadn't realized that Lisa cared. "Lisa, no one is to blame. It was an accident. A freaking accident! I know that. And really, I was the one who pushed her to go. But we both know that Jan wanted to go, or she wouldn't have gone. You can't blame yourself," Allison said.

"Look who's talking here," Lisa said, wiping away tears.

"We both wanted Jan to be happy," Allison said, "and Jan did what she wanted to do."

Lisa smiled. "Thanks. I guess you're right."

* * *

After the plane was refueled and the flight planning was done—and Lisa and Jan had a quick bite to eat—they were back in the air. The flight was smooth, and they soon landed at the private terminal in the Tri-Cities. They deplaned, and they and their luggage were quickly transported to the lobby.

"Hey, ladies! How was the flight?" they heard as they walked through the doors. It was Josh.

"Josh," Lisa said. She walked over to him, and they embraced. "Allison, you remember Josh, don't you?"

"Yes. Hi, Josh," Allison said.

"Yes, it's good seeing you, but I'm sorry it has to be under these sad circumstances," Josh said.

Allison gave him an affirmative nod and smiled, then looked to Lisa. "I guess I'll need to get someone to take me to the parking lot so I can get my car."

"It's all taken care of," Josh quickly answered. "The Uber driver is paid and waiting. We'll help you get your luggage in the car, and your passenger, Jan. The driver will take you to your car."

"Okay. Thank you. You and Lisa think of everything," Allison said.

"This is where we say goodbye . . . for now," Lisa said, her arms extended for a hug.

"Have a safe trip back," Allison answered as they embraced.

Lisa stepped back and said, "Thank you, Allison, for everything. If you need anything, don't hesitate to call me. Oh, I almost forgot." She reached into her handbag, took out an envelope, and handed it to Allison. "Read it when you get home. It's from Buckie."

Surprised, Allison took the envelope, stared at it, and then crammed it into her handbag. She said, "Will do. Thank you." Then she turned, walked to the Uber, and they headed to her car in the airport parking lot.

When she got home, she unpacked her car, and walked inside. She was exhausted. But being back home, reality set in as she unpacked her car and carried Jan's urn inside. She unsnapped the crate and took out the urn. She set it at the Christmas Tree. *You're home*, she thought. *You're home.*

Chapter 25

The next morning, Allison woke up feeling a dread because she knew she had a lot of work to do, including a lot of planning. She would have to tell people that Jan had died. She fixed herself a cup of coffee and started her day with a phone call to Jan's employer, Ms. Williams.

She spoke with Jan's boss, the company's owner, Ms. Williams, who shared with Allison that she suspected that Jan was deceased. "We saw on the international news that a tourist had drowned while vacationing at a resort in Belize. We were hoping that it was not Jan, but since we hadn't heard from her, and since she wasn't returning our phone calls, we were afraid and just waiting for confirmation. We were just hoping it wasn't her," Ms. Williams said. "I'm so sad. This breaks my heart. But thank you for letting us know."

"As her best friend, I'm taking care of things," Allison said.

"Well, if we can be of any assistance, please do not hesitate to ask. I remember that Jan mentioned she had a will that was handled by our company's attorney, Robert Caudill. That may help to know that," Ms. Williams said.

"Thank you," Allison said, ending the call.

Next on her call list was Preacher Hess. She dialed his number, but it went to his voicemail. She didn't leave a message, deciding instead to text him.

Allison: Hi Preacher Hess. Allison here. When u can call me.

There was a quick reply from Preacher Hess: will later

Okay, she thought, *next on my list, work.*

Allison worked part-time and had not reached out to her employer since the start of the holidays. She made the dreaded call to her boss and told him of Jan's passing. She said she would need more time off from work. Her boss was grateful to hear from her and was very sympathetic. He understood that she needed more time off from work but asked that she come in as soon as she could. Tax season had started, and clients were requesting that she help with their taxes.

As she was finishing the call, another call was coming in. It was Preacher Hess. "Yes, thank you! I will see you soon!" she said to her boss.

She clicked over to Preacher Hess's call and said, "Hi, this is Allison."

"Allison, it's so good to hear your voice. Preacher Hess here. How are ya doing?" he asked.

"Actually, I'm feeling better than I thought I would be considering I'm trying to get things taken care of for Jan," Allison said. "And that brings me to why I was reaching out to you. Do you think that you can conduct the service for Jan?"

"Of course," Preacher Hess answered without hesitation. "We can sit down and work out details and schedules. If it's okay, I can swing by later this evening. If that's good for you. Let's say six-thirty."

Allison looked at her watch and realized that it was already 2:30 p.m., and she hadn't even showered or changed out of her PJs. "Yes, six-thirty is fine. I appreciate your help," she said.

"I'll bring dinner," Preacher Hess said.

It took Allison by surprise since this was not a dinner date. "You don't really have to do that," she replied.

"No problem. We both have to eat, don't we?" he said with a snicker. "I'll see you at six-thirty." He hung up.

Guess I don't have a choice here, Allison thought. *And I've heard those words before.*

Next on her list was the attorney, Richard Caudill. She searched for his number and called his office. His receptionist answered.

"Hi, this is Allison Hurley. Is Mr. Caudill available?" Allison asked.

"No, Ms. Hurley. Mr. Caudill is out this afternoon. May I ask what this is regarding? Maybe I can be of some assistance to you," the receptionist said.

"Thank you, but this is regarding a client of his who recently passed. I have the documentation he needs in order to begin working on her estate," Allison answered. "She . . . she . . . died while on vacation. Her name is . . . was . . . I just need to make an appointment with him. He has also done some legal work for me."

"Oh, I see. Would the person who died be Jan Foster?" the receptionist asked.

Surprised, Allison answered, "Yes."

"We were contacted earlier by her employer and were told to expect your call. Mr. Caudill has availability tomorrow afternoon at three. Should I put you down for that time?" the receptionist asked.

"Yes," Allison replied.

"Okay, tomorrow, Friday, we will see you at three. Do you know where our office is located?" the receptionist said.

"Yes, thank you, I do. I'll see you tomorrow afternoon at three," Allison said.

After hanging up, Allison showered and dressed in preparation for Preacher Hess's arrival. She prepared the dining room by setting out place settings and opening a bottle of wine. *Maybe I can have a glass before he arrives*, she thought. *Doubt he drinks.*

Allison hadn't finished her glass of wine when she heard the doorbell. She walked to the door. "Hi, Preacher Hess. Please come in," she said as she opened the door.

"I'm sorry I'm early," Preacher Hess said, "but it didn't take as long as I thought it would to get the food. I hope that you like the jambalaya from The Tavern Restaurant. It's so cold outside, and I thought this would be perfect for a cold, snowy evening."

"Snowing?" Allison asked, peeping out the door.

"Just flurries. Not supposed to do much," Preacher Hess replied, closing the door behind him.

"The jambalaya is one of my favorite dishes from The Tavern. Sounds perfect! Bring it in here, and we will eat in the dining room," Allison said, directing him toward the dining room. "Need spoons, forks, bowls?"

"All of the above," Preacher Hess answered as he prepared the takeout on the table.

"Preacher Hess, would you like a glass of red wine?" Allison asked slowly.

He smiled and said, "Don't guess you have a beer?"

"Sorry, I'm not a beer drinker," Allison apologized.

"No problem. A glass of wine will work fine," he answered. "And please call me Steve."

"Steve?" Allison asked. "I never knew your name."

"Stephen Leroy Hess," Preacher Hess answered with a grin. "Now you know more about me than most!"

"Leroy?" Allison asked.

"Yes. It's not my favorite name, but I was named after my great-granddad. Thankfully, I'm called Steve," he said, and they both laughed.

Over dinner, Preacher Hess and Allison talked about everything except for what he was there to discuss. Allison found their conversation to be a wonderful distraction from the last few days' events.

As they finished eating, Allison poured herself another glass of wine. "Would you like more wine?"

"No, I'm good," Preacher Hess answered.

"Guess we need to talk about the service for Jan," Allison said slowly.

"Yes," Preacher Hess said. "What do you have in mind?"

"Well, I would like to have the service at the Abingdon Memorial, like we did for Lambert," Allison said.

"Okay, and did you have a day in mind?" Preacher Hess asked.

"Wasn't sure how it would fit in everyone's schedule," Allison said sadly.

"Let me suggest that we have the service a week from Sunday, and in the early afternoon if possible. That way, relatives, friends, and everyone wanting to attend will have time to plan. If that works for you. I'll contact Abingdon Memorial to see if it's available. Say for a two-thirty service? If we do an afternoon service, I'm sure some of the women from the church will be glad to help with set-up after the regular church service. Do you think that's okay?" Preacher Hess asked.

"Yes. I doubt there'll be a lot of people. Jan's got one brother, and they weren't really close. And he's really her only next of kin," Allison said. "So, if you could check on the time and let me know, I'll get the obituary and some pictures together."

"Will do. First thing tomorrow," Preacher Hess said.

"Thank you," Allison said with a loud sigh.

"I see you're tired, Allison, and it's getting late, so I guess I should go," he said.

"Sorry. With everything that has happened, I simply can't get enough sleep," Allison replied.

As they walked to the door, Preacher Hess looked at the Christmas tree. "I'd be happy to help you take down your Christmas tree," he offered. "Maybe tomorrow evening?"

Allison looked at the tree, but before she could answer, Preacher Hess took her hand, kissed it, and said, "I know that this isn't good timing, but when things settle down for you, I want to take you out to dinner. A date. I enjoy spending time with you, Allison, and it's not good to be alone."

Shocked, Allison abruptly said, "I always thought that you were married."

"I was until ten years ago. My wife died of breast cancer. It was a tough time for me, but it was God's will," Preacher Hess said.

"Preacher Hess—I mean, Steve—I'm sorry. I'm sure that was a difficult time for you," Allison said.

"Yes, it was," Preacher Hess said. "But please consider my invitation. I would like to take you out to a nice dinner sometime."

"Thank you," Allison said, not committing. "And be careful driving home."

Chapter 26

Allison woke the next morning thinking about Preacher Hess and him asking her on a date. *I can't really see me getting intimate with a preacher*, she thought, giggling as she got out of bed. She fixed herself a light breakfast and coffee, then started calling a few more people she knew were acquaintances or friends of Jan. After, she got dressed for her day.

Later, as she was headed out the door for her appointment, her cell phone beeped with a text message. It was from Preacher Hess.

Preacher Hess: Confirmed service a week from Sunday at 2:30. Will meet you there at 1:30 prior to service.

Allison texted: Thank you. I will get obituary and pictures to you.

Preacher Hess texted: Yes.

Allison texted: Thank you again!

Thank goodness he didn't ask me again about getting together this evening, Allison thought.

Allison arrived at Attorney Richard Caudill's office and was greeted by the receptionist.

"Hi, I'm Allison Hurley, and I have an appointment to see Mr. Caudill," she said.

"Yes. He's expecting you. Please follow me," the receptionist instructed. She walked down a hallway and stopped at a closed door. She knocked and opened the door. "Mr. Caudill, this is your three o'clock appointment, Ms. Hurley."

"Yes, thank you. And please close the door behind you. Ms. Hurley, please have a seat," Mr. Caudill instructed. "It's good to see you again."

"Thank you," Allison replied as she entered and sat down.

"How can I help you today?" Mr. Caudill asked.

"I guess you've heard about my friend Jan Foster?" Allison asked.

"Yes. She's a client of mine. Or was. Sad. I liked Jan. I also do corporate work for the company she worked for, and they called me and told that she drowned…on vacation?" Mr. Caudill asked.

"It was a freak accident. She was on a boat and tripped and fell overboard. She hit her head, and she drowned," Allison said, struggling to keep her composure.

"As I recall, you and she were best friends. Dated brothers. And those brothers disappeared…What now? Almost seven years? And they were never found," Mr. Caudill said.

Allison felt the blood drain from her face. Before she could answer, Mr. Caudill continued, saying, "Guess not. Ms. Hurley, are you okay? You look a little pale."

"Yes. It's just a very emotional time for me," Allison said, fighting back tears.

"I'm sure that it is," Mr. Caudill said. He handed her a bottle of water from his small office refrigerator.

"Thank you. I've brought documentation showing Jan's death and the cause of her death," Allison said, changing the subject. She handed him a large folder. "It has her death certificate, her passport, the police report, and some other paperwork."

"So, her death was established as an accident?" Mr. Caudill asked.

"Were you with her?"

"It was ruled an accident. And I wasn't with her. She made the trip on her own," Allison answered.

"She just up and went on a trip alone?" Mr. Caudill asked with surprise.

"Well, no. She was with a tour group. A local tour group," Allison said, feeling like she was being cross-examined.

"Oh, I see," Mr. Caudill said, flipping through the paperwork. "Well, this paperwork is complete. It appears all the T's are crossed and all the I's are dotted. I pulled her file earlier. Did you know that you're named in her will?"

"Me?" Allison asked, totally surprised.

"Yes. You know those brothers' insurance policies had the two of you named as beneficiaries. If the brothers are not located or pronounced dead, they can't be used for seven years. She left her policy to you in case it was ever paid, and she was deceased. And according to the dates, the seven years end in February of this year. That's in the very near future," Mr. Caudill said, looking directly at Allison, seeming to seek a reaction.

Allison swallowed hard. "So, what are you saying?" she asked calmly.

"I'm saying that the two million dollars that would have gone to Jan will go to you," Mr. Caudill said sternly.

"I didn't know that she did that," Allison said defensively. "I had no idea."

"Well, I'll keep in touch, especially since you also have a policy in the same amount," Mr. Caudill said. "The FBI never figured out what happened to them—the brothers—did they?"

Allison kept her composure and answered, "No, not that I know of. The FBI didn't find anything . . . anything that they would share with Jan or me. They questioned us several times, but we had nothing to tell them. So, I do not know what they did or did not find."

"Interesting," Mr. Caudill replied. "Really strange how two men just disappear from an airport."

"Is there anything else that I need to do or provide you with so you can start on Jan's estate?" Allison asked, changing the subject.

"No. Not at this time. I appreciate you bringing this paperwork to me. I will start getting her estate settled," Mr. Caudill answered.

Allison stood up and walked to the door.

Mr. Caudill said, "I'm sorry for your loss, Ms. Hurley. I hope that this New Year ends up better for you than the way it started."

Allison turned and smiled. "Thank you. I hope so, too!"

Allison left the building and walked to her car. When she got inside, she had to just sit for a moment and compose herself. She thought, *What a jerk! Wonder if he does know that they're alive?*

Suddenly, she heard a soft, angelic whisper, as if someone was sitting next to her.

Jackson and Brandon are dead.

Allison felt chills race down her spine. It took a minute for her to catch her breath. *Yes,* she thought, *Jackson and Brandon are dead.*

Chapter 27

The next few days were busy for Allison. She contacted Jan's employer again, who graciously wrote the obituary, and sent notices out to friends and all the local media outlets. Allison had gone to work for a couple of days but found it difficult to concentrate. But it did help take her mind off things.

Soon, the days turned into a week, and she was getting dressed to go to Jan's service. She carried the travel bag with Jan's urn. She set it in the front seat of her car and fastened the seat belt around it to secure it.

"On this cloudy, cold day, this is our last ride together, Jan. I'm going to miss you," Allison said out loud, tears filling her eyes, and then she got in her car and pulled out of her driveway.

She arrived at Abingdon Memorial Gardens at exactly 1:30 p.m. She gathered the travel bag and walked inside. Preacher Hess and some of the church members were already there.

"Hey, you're right on time," Preacher Hess greeted her.

"Yes, and you're early," Allison said with a smile.

"Just thought that I would get here and make sure all was set up," Preacher Hess replied. "You have Jan with you?"

"Yes. Here," Allison said. She set the travel bag down on the table next to Jan's oversized pictures. She unzipped the bag and removed the urn.

"Wow! I've never seen such a nice urn," Preacher Hess remarked. "I've done a lot of services, but this is the nicest urn that I've ever seen.

It's engraved. Looks like her name and her birth and death dates are all engraved in gold."

Allison just looked at the urn. *Yup, gold,* she thought.

"Who do we recognize for providing her this care?" Preacher Hess asked.

Allison didn't answer. She just looked at Preacher Hess.

"So, is it a secret close friend?" Preacher Hess asked quietly.

"No. Actually, the resort made all the arrangements, and I guess they wanted to provide the best for the family . . . under the circumstances," Allison answered.

"Oh, I see," Preacher Hess replied. "They certainly did not spare any expense. Why, even the travel bag is trimmed in gold and folds into a smaller bag."

"Yes. I'll take the travel bag back with me. It doesn't seem to be needed anymore," Allison remarked.

"'Love Always' is signed on her urn," Preacher Hess said. "Don't you find it odd that the resort engraved that on an urn?"

Without missing a beat, Allison replied, "No, not really. The resort believes love never ends."

"In a way, it doesn't," Preacher Hess confirmed. "God's love through His son, Jesus, lasts for an eternity."

* * *

Guests arrived on time, and soon the service began. Just as the service started, the sun broke through the clouds, and it gleamed brightly through the high stained-glass windows for the entire service. Preacher Hess was gracious and a comforting message confirming that Jan was in a better place.

As the service came to a conclusion, Allison said a silent, thoughtful prayer. *Jan, thank you for being my best friend. You were always there for me, and I wasn't always there for you, and I'm sorry. But I always loved you as a sister. I pray that you are at peace. I'll always love you…and miss you. May God's love be with you. Amen.*

As guests left, many stopped to shake Preacher Hess's hand and thank him for his wonderful service. Jan's brother introduced himself to Allison and thanked her for taking care of things. To show his appreciation, he handed an envelope of money to Preacher Hess.

After everyone had gone, Allison remained seated, and Preacher Hess sat down beside her.

"It was a very good service, and thank you," Allison said. "Jan would've been pleased. I was surprised by the number of people who showed up."

"Yes, it was a good group, and they seemed to care very much about Jan. She must have had genuine friends. Knowing more about Jan made me know more about you. Reading her bio, it told me a lot about you, Allison. It explained to me how the two of you were such great friends," Preacher Hess said.

"Jan and I shared a lot. We had the same morals and values, and we loved the same things in life, including the pursuit of happiness. We could talk about anything and understand how the other one felt. It was a special friendship. And…now…she's gone," Allison replied.

"Gone, but in a better place and never forgotten," Preacher Hess said.

"Thank you again, Preacher Hess," Allison said. "And here is a small token of my thanks." She handed him an envelope with money inside.

"Steve. Remember?" Preacher Hess asked. "And you do not owe me anything."

"Yes. Steve. Just a small way of saying thank you. If you want, just give it to the church. Do I need to stay and do anything more here?" Allison said.

"Thank you, and no. You go on home, and I'll finish up here," he said. "Do you want company later? I can come by around seven-thirty, right after our Sunday night service?"

"That's very kind of you. If you don't mind, though, I think that I'll go on home and just be alone," Allison answered. "I hope that you understand."

"Totally," Preacher Hess replied. "But call me if you do need anything, okay?"

"I will. And thank you again. I couldn't have gotten through this without your help," Allison said, and then she stood up and walked out the side entrance. She headed to her car and looked back as if to say one more goodbye.

* * *

By the time Allison got home, it was cloudy again, and very cold. She set her handbag and the travel bag on the sofa. *I think I'll change, fix a hot toddy, and take down the Christmas tree. Guess it's about time to do that*, she thought.

Allison removed all the Christmas decorations and lights, and the only ornament remaining on the tree was the ornament that she had given Jan as a Christmas gift. As she gently removed it, she heard a whisper that she recognized. It was the soft, angelic whisper she'd heard earlier.

I'm at peace. Go find yours.

The words paralyzed Allison. She was jolted back into reality by the ding of her cell phone. She went to get her cell phone from her handbag and accidentally knocked it over. Everything spilled out on the floor, including the letter from Lambert and the envelope that Lisa had handed to her at the Tri-Cities Airport. *Oh my*, she thought, *I forgot about the letter!*

She picked up the unopened letter and the phone at the same time. She had a text message.

Preacher Hess: Just checking on you. U okay?

She put down the phone and opened the letter with trembling hands.

My Dear Allison,
I never had the chance to tell you just how truly, truly sorry I am that you've gone through such sadness because of me . . . and Winston. Please find it in your heart to forgive me. I am here. This is sent to you with love that never ends . . . and peace.

Peace, she thought. Allison read and reread the note. *Yes . . . I want my peace back.*

Allison took Jan's ornament and the note and placed them in the travel bag.

She slowly picked up Lambert's letter and tossed it in the fireplace. It burned quickly. She watched it as it burn.

She picked up her phone and texted Preacher Hess.

Allison: Ok. Thank you for all you have done.

Allison browsed through her recent calls and tapped a familiar number. She got Lisa's voicemail and left a message. "Hey, Lisa. Allison here. I have a big favor to ask of you. I need a one-way ticket to Belize. I'm going to be staying at that really nice, peaceful resort, and I won't be returning anytime soon."

About the Author

Jan Howery, a native of Southwest Virginia, writes with an Appalachian influence. Her many writings include "The Daisy Flower Garden," featured in the anthology *Broken Petals*, and "The Devil Behind the Barn" featured in the anthology *These Haunted Hills: A Collection of Short Stories*, "The Straight Back Chair," in *These Haunted Hills Book 2*, "Right or Wrong," featured in *Wild Daisies*, "The Love of Daisies" in *Scattered Flowers*, and "Dreams of Being a Teacher" in *Daffodil Dreams*. Other writings include fashion and health columns for the Appalachian regional magazine for women, *Voice Magazine for Women*.

www.ingramcontent.com/pod-product-compliance
Lightning Source LLC
LaVergne TN
LVHW091003080826
845145LV00003B/1105

* 9 7 8 1 9 5 4 9 7 8 8 9 8 *